WiLD
SONG

WILD SONG

JANIS MACKAY

Piccadilly
PRESS

First published in Great Britain in 2015 by Piccadilly Press
Northburgh House, 10 Northburgh Street, London EC1V 0AT
www.piccadillypress.co.uk

A CIP catalogue record for this book is available
from the British Library.

ISBN: 9781848124424

3 5 7 9 10 8 6 4 2

Typeset by Palimpsest Book Production Ltd, Falkirk, Stirlingshire

Printed and bound by Clays Ltd, St Ives Plc

Piccadilly Press is part of the Bonnier Publishing Group
www.bonnierpublishing.com

To my mother, Mary Mackay
who encouraged me to sing, dance and walk on the
Wild side.

And to the Secret Readers of George Heriot's
School, Edinburgh:
Mrs Elaine Clarke, English teacher, and her pupils;
Grace Dobson, Freya Groves, Paul Ferguson,
Jeremy Saville, Rory Tait and Ayesha Qasim.
For reading and critiquing the first draft of
Wild Song.
Thank You.

Chapter One

His whole body jerks like he's been kicked awake. But he isn't awake, he's dreaming. He's back in the sea. It's always the sea. A thick grey wall of water looms up. It's moving towards him, towering over him. Now it's falling on him. Another rears, then another – great crashing waves.

Until the seventh giant wave changes shape. It's not a grey wall now but a boat, tossed like a toy. The boat has gone, swallowed into the sea. Hands stretch up through the churning water. Fingers reach, grasp, then vanish. Then the hands are gone. So is the sea.

The pounding is his heart. His eyes stare wildly up at the ceiling. It is the ceiling, not the cruel sky. He's in a bed, not a boat. It's a dream, that's all it is – a bad dream, he tells himself over and over, till the room stops rocking.

Go back to sleep, Niilo. You are not going to drown.

* * *

1

So, I'm not a great sleeper. And it's getting worse. I'm scared to fall asleep in case the waves roll over me and the bed turns into a boat. To fight the nightmares I lie on the hard floor. I don't bother about blankets. It's uncomfortable, cold, but that way I stay awake for hours. I lie with my eyes closed, listening to the sounds of the night. I like how the trams rattle, ring their bell, then fade away. I hear barking dogs, the squeal of car tyres, the wail of far-off sirens. I lie on the floor in the night and invent my own world. I call it The Capsule. In it I make the sirens howling wolves, barking dogs become growling bears, the rattles of trams are pounding hooves of reindeer. And I'm far from Helsinki – I'm running with mighty elk in dark forests . . .

But sleep is a hunter. It catches me. Because next thing Mum is crying over me, and holding me. 'Niilo, oh, Niilo,' she sobs.

She tries to slip a pillow under my head but I push her away. The dream has fled and I'm wide awake. I bark at her like a dog.

'Don't,' she whines.

I grab whatever is closest – a book – and fling it at the wall. She screams and shields her face, but I wasn't aiming for her. The early morning light catches her eyes and I see she's scared of me. She backs away, but doesn't leave like I want her to. She stands at the door, shaking.

'This can't go on,' she says. Her voice is shaking now. I'm ready to punch my fist on the floor when she cries,

'Stop it!' There's something different in her voice. The shaking has gone. She doesn't look scared, she looks guilty. She lifts her hands up, like she's innocent. 'Don't blame me, Niilo. I did my best.' She's got tears in her eyes. 'I thought this was the way to manage. I don't know what else to do.'

But she still doesn't leave.

So I laugh. I want to tell her to take a chill pill. Relax. Just eight more months, then she'll never have to set eyes on the problem son any more. Because as soon as I hit fourteen, I'm out of here. *Adios*. Off I go! World get ready, cos here I come.

Except I don't do long sentences. 'Get out,' is all I say.

But she doesn't. It's like she is trying to tell me something but can't get the words out. 'Niilo?' I don't look at her. I'm looking for the remote control. Music. That's what I need. 'You do have to go to school,' she says. 'It's the law.' She's hovering at my bedroom door, fumbling with the handle but not turning it. 'There are . . . schools, Niilo. Special places that can help you.'

I find the remote and flick on the music. Mum is chattering on, but I turn the music up so loud it's thumping off the walls, and her mouth is like a fish, opening and closing with no sound coming out. She shakes her head and goes.

Then I sleep. The dreams don't find me in the day. I sleep till two. An hour later I'm down at the market. It's only April, still cold, but that doesn't stop the tourists.

3

There's a crowd of them swarming around the reindeer furs – something sick to me about a pile of skin and fur for sale. 'A bargain at one hundred and fifty euros,' the man at the stall is screeching. 'Take a piece of genuine Finland home for only one hundred and fifty euros.'

There's a woman stroking the dead deer. I slink in behind her, silent as a hunter. And there it is, right under my nose: the woman's bag, open for business. I spy the purse inside, black leather and fat. The crowd are all gaping at the dead reindeer. I dip my hand in. 'It is very beautiful,' the woman says, practically purring. 'We do not have such creatures in Japan.'

I linger in that bag a second too long. My fingers brush the soft leather, I unclip the clasp, pull out a wad of notes, then all hell breaks out. 'It's him!' somebody shouts. The woman screams and spins round but she's too late – her cash is deep in my pocket. She tries to whack me with her bag and I duck. 'Catch him!' the man at the stall shouts. 'Catch the thief!'

I take off, zipping through the crowds like an acrobat. Zigzag slalom-style always confuses people. I feel somebody's hand pull at my jacket. I wriggle and squirm free. I hear my jacket rip. I dive into a group of kids, out on some trip.

'Grab him!' someone shouts. 'Him with the long black hair. Get him!'

Forget slalom. I bolt through the crowds, knocking kids and old ladies aside. A blurred sea of shocked faces rushes past. I bang into a stall of woollen hats. They go flying. A woman swears. Someone tries to snatch at my chain belt but I side-skip, like a boxer. There's something thrilling about being chased. Everyone is yelling and grabbing at me but I'm fast. Slippery like oil. I duck again, then dart over the road, in front of a bus. The driver blasts the horn and slams on the brakes but I'm safely on the other side, feeling like I just crossed the river rapids.

All my pursuers are standing shaking their fists – waiting for the signal to cross the road. I speed up a side street away from the market.

Two minutes later I'm on the metro, heading home with one hundred and thirty-five euros in my pocket. I sit back and try and relax, but there's a river of sweat running down my back and my heart is pounding like a drum. The metro clatters under Helsinki.

That was close. Too close.

Chapter Two

I slip into my room and stash the cash in a lunch box under my bed. I'm starving. I could spend some euros on takeaway pizza but I'm saving up for the big adventure. So I raid the fridge instead.

I cram cheese into my mouth so fast I can't taste it, but Mum and Dad and Tuomas, my little brother, are all sitting there, at the kitchen table. They're staring at me so weirdly I can hardly swallow the stuff. Something is up. Dad is eyeing me coldly and Mum keeps running her fingers through her hair. It was always tense in this house, but now it's really bad. Even Tuomas, who is usually a chatterbox, doesn't say anything. There's an atmosphere and I don't know why, but it's making me uneasy.

Dad isn't all quiet like he used to be. He's holding Mum's hand and she's doing her shaking thing again. 'Do you see what you are doing to your mother?' he says, trying not to shout. 'You are making her ill.' He's patting her hair. 'You have no respect for us.' He's working hard to keep his voice steady. 'Your little brother looks up to you.' Dad's losing it now. He's raising his voice. I spit out the cheese. 'You don't even look at him. Living with you is like living with a monster. This can't go on, Niilo. We can do no more.'

I laugh and grab a can of Coke from the fridge.

'I am warning you, Niilo. This can't go on.'

I'm feeling scared and I don't know why. I growl and stomp into my room.

That's where I am, two days later, lying on the carpet listening to CrashMetal turned up as loud as it will go, the bass thudding right through my bones. I don't make it to the end of the song. The doorbell goes. That's unusual, so I notice it – even with the thrashing music I can hear it buzz. I sit up and I've got this cold feeling. For no reason I suddenly feel shivery. Next thing, I can hear Mum crying out. Something is wrong.

I grab the remote and turn the music down. Now I can hear the voices of my parents. Urgent, hushed voices. Then the buzz of the doorbell again, more insistent this time. I jump to my feet, like I have to be ready, and I hear the front door being opened. Muffled voices. High and low voices. Then the hurried sound of Mum's footsteps. Something *is* up.

Next thing, my bedroom door flies open and there's Mum, standing in the doorway, her hair dishevelled. Black streaked mascara stains her face. 'I'm sorry,' she sobs. She tries to hug me but I push me away, my heart pounding fast. I can hear rapid voices coming from the hallway and I feel a panic grip at my gut. I dive under the bed and grab at my stash of cash. 'I'm sorry, Niilo,' Mum is saying over and over, 'but I had to.'

Sorry for what? Had to what? The entire contents of my lunch box spills over the floor and I clutch at the notes and stuff them up my sleeve. I'm only thirteen. This isn't the plan. Well, too bad. Something tells me it's time to split. Now!

I push back the bed and bolt out of the room. Mum runs after me, still crying – sorry – sorry. A slow-motion film comes on in my head.

Making. Everything. Technicolor.

Take for ever.

Dad is standing in the doorway of the study, looking down at the ground. He won't make eye contact. There's a large black suitcase by the front door. Beside it are two men in dark clothes. Tall men. Square jaws. Serious expressions. Behind them, a fist mark on the pale yellow wall. *My* fist mark. From some outburst – I try to remember which one. Behind me Mum is still sobbing, 'I'm sorry.' Over and over. 'I'm *sorry!*'

I stare at the men. At first I think they are police, as if I always knew they'd catch up with me. It feels like I've always been waiting for this moment – that it was always coming – though I don't care as much as I thought I would. But they don't look like police.

'We gave you everything,' Mum is crying. She's trying

to grab me by the arm. 'This is a chance to start over, Niilo. They said it was better not to tell you, until the day. It's for your own good. It's a nice place you are going to. A special school. They will help you. Don't think badly of me. And it's not for ever.'

'Not for ever, Niilo,' Dad echoes, like a puppet. It's like the chorus of a song. *Not for ever, Niilo.*

'Hi, Niilo. I'm Sam,' one of the men says, looking straight at me. His voice is strong, deep, his gaze steady. He nods to the side. 'This is Vilho.'

Who are these men if they are not police? Why are they coming towards me? I push my mum aside and lash out at the wall. And it hits me in a flash: the black suitcase is for *me* – I am being taken away. I dive for the door but a strong hand wraps fast around my arm. I kick the suitcase over, but these men are strong. They've done this kind of thing before. Doesn't mean I don't fight, and wriggle and yell like hell.

But in three minutes flat I'm gone from the house. And so are the laces off my trainers. And they find the secret pocket, and in it my knife, and the cigarettes and lighter. As they escort me into the car the cash falls out of my sleeve. The one called Sam scoops up the notes and runs back to the house while Vilho holds my arm. I watch from the car window, watch Sam hand over the money to Dad, watch Dad take the money as he stands on the doorstep looking totally bewildered. Then Dad is waving at me, the wad of cash in his hand. I glare at him, then look away.

Sam drives. Vilho sits in the back next to me. None of this feels real – it's like I'm in a film. I can feel tears stinging my eyes. My teeth are chattering. I can't stop them, but there's something thrilling about the speed of it all too. The car is purring through the leafy neighbourhood, then out onto the main road into central Helsinki. Sam drives faster out on the highway.

'Your mother couldn't cope any more,' Vilho says. 'You are lucky though, Niilo. You're going to the Wild School. We don't always do it this way, kidnap-style, but your mum thought you'd run away if you knew. Sorry for the hasty exit.'

Sam laughs and winks at me in the rear-view mirror. 'It's not a bad place we're taking you to. Relax, buddy, it's going to be fine.'

I imagine wild animals, lions and tigers, brown bears and herds of stampeding buffalo.

'It's on an island,' Sam says as the car approaches the harbour. The market stalls by the harbour are in full swing and I'm picturing reindeer skins. I'm trying not to think about the sea. Ahead there is a small ferryboat with its ramp down. The car heads straight for it.

I'm starting to seriously panic. There are a lot of things I don't like, but the sea is the main one. I bite my lip, hard, as the car nears the ferry. I can taste blood.

'The Wild School has its very own island. No expense spared,' Sam says. 'For the bad boy, eh?' He revs the engine as the car rolls onto the ramp.

The metal structure clatters with the weight of the car and I think I might wet myself. I can't believe this is happening. I clamp my eyes tight shut – but I've got to see what's going on, so I have to open them again. And it's only the ferryman plus Sam, Vilho and me on the boat. The black car is the only car rolling over the ramp.

Once we're in the belly of the boat Sam turns off the engine. The car sways. We stay inside. 'We'll sit in the car,' he says. 'It's a pretty short journey.' The ferry clunks as the ramp comes up. Then it's off.

The car lurches from side to side. There are still chunks of ice in the sea, and the boat breaks it up, bumping, growling. I clutch at the car seat and panic rises in my throat, like puke.

'Bumpy ride,' Sam calls out. 'Hang on and keep breathing.' I'm groaning, I can't help it. 'Give him a bag, Vilho, for God's sake,' Sam shouts.

But it is too late for any bag. I throw up over Vilho's black trousers.

'Jesus,' he cries, edging away. 'Get him out of the car.'

Next thing, I'm clinging onto the rails of the ferryboat, groaning and kicking at the lifebuoy. Again and again I throw up. Vomit spins into the sea spray as Helsinki lurches and dips behind us and ice splits and crunches below. Vilho is at my back, clutching at my hoodie, just in case I'm about to hurl myself overboard. Through the tears and sick and terror I can see a small island grow bigger.

Sam staggers across the deck with a towel. 'Wipe yourself clean,' he shouts. 'We're almost there.'

When we arrive at the island the car rolls off the ramp and clatters up a dirt track that doesn't look made for cars. After a couple of minutes and hundreds of pine trees, the car stops and the two men – one on either side – escort me out of the car. If I didn't feel so queasy I might have felt like a celebrity.

'We walk this last bit,' Vilho says, groaning. He sounds pretty ill too.

My knees keep buckling. Sam and Vilho hold me up. I'm vaguely aware of a blur of trees. And someone shouting in the distance. I see some hens. I hear a dog bark. I see a wooden bench. We stop in front of the bench.

'Look what it says on it,' Sam says. '*Welcome to the Wild School.*' Moaning, I sink onto the bench. We all do. 'Make the most of it here,' Sam says. Then he nudges me and smiles. 'Wild child!'

'Yeah, blooming wild, right enough,' Vilho says.

I don't look at him, but can see the stain of puke over his trousers. The smell makes me feel sick all over again. Groaning, I lift my head. In front of us, between a grove of pine trees, is a large red-brick building. Is that *it*? The Wild School? It doesn't look wild!

'You get to do all kinds of adventurous stuff here,' Sam says.

But I'm already determined to make nothing of it. I frown, like I am not interested in the large building and adventurous stuff. But inside me a small victory is pulsing away. Because I crossed the sea. And survived.

'It's all right for you,' Vilho says. 'You get to stay here. We've got to turn round and go back! Could you not have chosen a better day?'

I look at him. I haven't spoken up till now. I cough. I can feel the sick stick in my throat. I cough again, then say three husky words. 'I didn't choose.'

After that, I don't speak for a long time.

Chapter Three

I arrive on a Friday. Film night. 'Welcome to the Wild School,' some big man with stubble on his chin says, thrusting out his hand. I don't look at him. I don't shake his hand. The big man keeps up his positive script even though my lip is curled up and I stink of vomit. 'You're lucky, Niilo. You're just in time for a movie. Do you like movies?'

Stupid question. It depends on the movie. But I don't say anything. The big man keeps on. 'You're going to like this one.'

As it happens, I did. That night, in the games hall, they showed a film called *Braveheart* where some guy got hanged, drawn and quartered, but even when he was being killed he shouted, '*Freedom!*' Most of the boys in the games hall yelled 'Freedom!' too. All the boys were crazy – I worked that out in about two minutes flat. I'd been brought to some loony bin. After the film I scrawled the word 'freedom' over the wall of my tiny room with a black felt pen. Freedom, I decided that first night, was the only thing worth living for.

The drowning nightmare came back, full-tilt. It was the ferry trip that did it, and my new room. The room was small and kind of bleak. It smelt of bleach. Every time I closed my eyes I felt woozy, like I was back on that boat. I tried not to fall asleep, but I couldn't fight it. Next thing, the familiar lurch hit me, like a punch in the gut. A thick grey wall of water loomed high, then charged at me. Waves the size of mountains came at me. The next wave turned into a boat. It reared up, then sank. Hands thrashing, grasping, clutching, then that horrible scream . . .

I woke up in the middle of the night, gasping, feeling like I was drowning. I didn't know where I was. I grabbed at the duvet, then I kicked it off me. In a flash it all came back to me. I was in the Wild School – this small room with a bed, a table, a chair and a rug on the wooden floor was my new home.

The Wild School wasn't *called* a prison. It was called a Wild *school*. But there was nothing else on the small island apart from loads of trees and bushes and stones and fields – and it was one of these Finnish islands that you can walk round in about twenty minutes. A rock in the ocean, surrounded by sea. Great! Even though they made a big deal about saying the Wild School wasn't a prison, it certainly felt like one. After all, I couldn't just leave! And like I said, some of the boys were seriously crazy. No girls – just bad boys who made a lot of noise. The staff looked mostly okay, but they were paid to be okay. Anyway, they got on a boat and went home after their shift. They got days off too. And apparently they were black belts in karate, some of them.

In my room, that first day, I kicked the walls and managed to break a bone in my toe. The school nurse put a splint on it and gave me a cup of hot chocolate. She was one of the few women on the island, not pretty, but she had nice hair that smelt of lemon shampoo. She said the same thing as Sam. *Make the most of it here.* Like it was the Wild School script.

Not for ever, Niilo. Make the most of it here, Niilo! Wild child!

Next, I punched the walls. I was gasping for a cigarette. This place was bristling with rules. No drugs. No alcohol. No cigarettes. No violence. No weapons. No internet. No mobile phones. I bruised my hands black and blue till they put me into a room with soft walls.

For three days and nights I wouldn't come out. They gave me water in a plastic cup to drink. They gave me bread and cheese. They gave me a bucket to pee in. I did, then tipped it over so the place stank, but I didn't care. Mostly I slept. Until after three or four days the door clicked open and the same guy with the stubble chin stepped in.

'Right, Niilo,' he said in a no-messing tone of voice, 'let's start work then, shall we?'

16

Some of his henchmen came and frogmarched me off to work in the woodwork studio. To make great things out of wood! That's what they told me. Fat chance. I stood in the huge wooden shed all day, with my hands in my pockets. No way was I going to work. It was pointless.

The woodwork teacher was a guy called Marko. He had a very hairy beard which was pretty gross. 'Let's start you on something simple, shall we, Niilo?' he said, like I was stupid. He was waving the branch of a tree around. 'You can start by stripping the bark off this,' he said. I shook my head and ignored him.

While the other boys did what Marko told them, like sheep, I hung about near the window and gazed out at the sea. I had my own agenda. This was an island – it wasn't big, but it was still surrounded by sea. I could see a white goat tied to a rope. Even that goat was a prisoner. While the boys in the room chattered and laughed and sanded wood and threw sawdust at each other, I stood on my own. I turned my back on them and forced myself to watch the sea. I stared and counted to one hundred, even though I felt terrified. The sea had so much power.

I did this for a few days and nobody forced me to do woodwork. Marko tried, that was for sure. Every day he came up with some 'interesting' task, like sanding chopping boards. 'The boys are making useful things from wood,' he told me, like I was interested. 'You know we had one boy here, he's moved on since, but he made a rocking horse. He discovered a real talent for woodwork. You might too, Niilo.' I looked over his shoulder, putting on my total boredom face.

Marko brought me books on woodwork. He fetched me wooden bowls and stuff and I was supposed to feel how warm and friendly the wood felt! I shook my head. Or I ignored him. Another time Marko tried to put a piece of sandpaper in my hand. 'It's rough to the touch,' he said, 'but it makes the wood smooth.' I crushed it and dropped it and stubbed it out like it was a cigarette. 'Oh well,' he said, 'it seems you're not even prepared to give it a go.' He didn't try again.

After eight days I could stare at the sea for a count of five thousand. A huge ferry passed every day, sailing from Helsinki to Stockholm. I know that because Marko told me. 'I see you're interested in the ferryboats, Niilo,' he said, trying to play it all friendly. 'The winter ice has pretty much melted now. With luck we'll have a good summer, eh, Niilo?'

I ignored him, just watching the ferry as it glided over the surface of the sea, like a floating town. Sooner or later I'd make my getaway. I pictured myself on that huge ferry, off to Sweden. I planned on doing mime on the streets there. I'd seen guys in Helsinki stand still as statues. All they did was dress up, put a hat in front of them, keep still, and they earned a fortune. I was pretty good at keeping still too.

'I can't get him to do anything.' That was Marko. I overheard him talking to the boss, Mr Stubble. I was leaning against the wall in the corridor at the time, being invisible. Marko was shaking his head and shrugging: the body language of defeat. That felt like a small victory, seeing him all sagging in his big shoulders. 'With the other boys it's fine. We make a good team. We crack jokes. I can get them to work. Some of them are making bread-boards. But with Niilo, nothing works.' He sounded deflated, poor guy. 'Niilo doesn't care. He ignores me and just stares out the window. He never speaks. He never takes his hands out of his pockets. He sneers at the boys that do work, and it's getting so that the boys who used to like woodwork are saying: Why do we have to work when Niilo doesn't?'

So I was taken off Marko's team. Next day I was walked out to the garden and they gave me a one-to-one worker.

Hannu.

Chapter Four

'Heard you're pretty skilled in picking things,' Hannu said. He slung weeds into the basket like rapid fire.

For the first time in days I felt something like pride. But Hannu left it at that. He filled his basket with weeds while I kept my hands stuffed deep in my pockets. We were in a field at the back of the Wild School, some vegetable plot or something. I hadn't exactly been helping, just standing about. I didn't speak and wondered whether I still could. But hours later, in my room, the compliment came back to me. *Heard you're pretty skilled in picking things.* Skilled. It was pathetic, but I ran it over and over in my mind. Skilled! I, Niilo, was skilled. Never mind he meant picking pockets. He hadn't called me a thief. He'd called me *skilled*. I liked that.

Didn't mean I actually started working, but I watched Hannu down on his knees working. I watched the way he dug his fingers under the earth to twist out a weed. I watched the dark soil crumble. It was May and Hannu said how we could start planting stuff soon: flowers and veg. He always said 'we' even though he did all the work. 'Hands are amazing, aren't they?' Hannu brought his hands out of the earth and spread his fingers. 'They can work. They can play guitar, they can hold, and . . .' He didn't look at me. He kept staring at his grimy hands. Suddenly he clenched his hands into fists and brought them down hard into the soil. 'They can hurt.' He was silent for a moment. I didn't move. Then he grabbed a fistful of soil and stood up. I stepped back fast. 'If this was snow,' he said, 'you and me could have a snowball fight.' Then he loosened his grasp of the dirt and it ran out of his clutch. 'But winter is over.' Hannu laughed, then.

I felt my heart race. I didn't know what to make of him. I didn't know if that was a mocking laugh, or what. I couldn't tell. But when Hannu turned his back to tip the weeds into the compost I bent down and grabbed some soil. I don't know why I did that. But something about the way he was going on about it made dirt into something magical, and I wanted to feel it. It was clammy. I shot up before Hannu turned back and I stuffed the black crumbly earth into my pocket where I rubbed at it.

That night the image of Hannu's strong hands pounding the earth came back to me. And I still had that tiny piece of soil. I put it on my pillow and rubbed my face in it, smeared it over my cheeks, like I was getting ready for some war dance. I liked the feel of the earth against my cheek.

21

'Let's walk round the island,' Hannu said the next morning. My face was still dirty, and he must have noticed because he nodded and smiled. Then he looked around and flung his arms wide. 'The Wild School owns this whole island. It's not big – one of the archipelago's smaller jewels.'

I shrugged. Maybe he thought I didn't know what *archipelago* meant. Even if I didn't, I wasn't going to let on.

'A sea dotted with islands,' Hannu explained, sweeping his arm to the side, as if scattering islands about. 'There are thousands of them out there, Niilo, though most are little more than rocks sticking out of the water. But there are big islands out there too.' Hannu scratched his head, like he was clicking through to a computer in his brain. 'Over two hundred, so I heard.'

After that little lecture Hannu beckoned for me to follow him. As long as I didn't have to go too close to the sea, I didn't care where I went. He strode off, along the side of the field he'd been weeding, and I slouched behind.

He was talking as if I was right next to him. 'Over by the field there we keep a couple of goats. We might try milking them one of these days. And these are birch trees, Niilo. Their leaves are just about to come out.' He waved to a clump of trees at the edge of the field. 'But I suppose you know what a birch tree is.' Then he cut into the wood and glanced behind to make sure I was following.

I was kind of curious, and Hannu wasn't the worst staff member at the Wild School. He had something rule-breaking about him. Maybe it was his black hair, which was kind of long. Or it was because of his earring. Or maybe it was that he played bass guitar in a band – I know that because he told me. I'd even heard of the band.

It was gloomy in the woods. 'And at the edge of the wood there are lots of pine trees,' he shouted. 'Take a deep breath and you'll smell the pine resin. I love that smell.' We reached the edge of the wood and came to a ragged field with nettles, little spring flowers and bushes. 'Ever eaten a fresh nettle?' Hannu said, whipping the top off a nettle and popping it into his mouth. I screwed up my face but he just laughed. 'Do it quick and you don't get stung. They are bursting with iron.' He snatched up another nettle top and offered it to me. 'They're not only good for you, they taste good too.' I shook my head – nettles weren't exactly my idea of a snack – so Hannu ate it. Then he pulled a paper bag out of his pocket and picked a few more nettles, snapping the tops off. 'I'll give them to the cook,' he said when he was done. 'They're really tasty in soup. Maybe you can have them for supper.' I shrugged, like I didn't care what I had. I didn't even eat in the dining hall – I ate in my room and I liked it that way. *Liked* is too strong a word. *Preferred*.

With his bag of precious nettles he set off. 'We're explorers,' he called out, striding over the springy bushes. 'When you know where to look there's a lot of really tasty wild food.' Hannu laughed and winked at me. 'Good for the Wild School, eh? To have wild food?'

I shrugged. I wasn't totally sure what he meant by wild

food. Maybe he read my confused expression, because he went on, 'There's red sorrel, ground elder, wild herbs, mushrooms, berries, and that's just for starters.' Suddenly he pounced on a few boring looking leaves at his feet, like he'd just stumbled on gold. 'Look, Niilo, these here are dandelion leaves.' He pulled a couple of leaves from a clump and popped them in his mouth. 'It's amazing what you can find,' he said, picking some more and handing them to me. 'Want to try?' I stared at the small bright green leaves in his open palm. I did want them, but I shook my head. 'Suit yourself,' he said, and tossed them into his mouth. Still chewing on his rabbit food he looked at me quizzically. 'You've got the north in you,' he said, then strode on.

I followed him, thinking he was kind of crazy. What did he mean – the north in me? I hurried after him.

Suddenly he swung round and looked straight at me. 'It's like a hunger for wild places, northern places.' He laughed, like he was embarrassed saying that. 'I call it "wild hunger". I see it in you, Niilo, because I know it in myself.' He laughed again, and carried on walking.

We reached a bit where the land sloped downwards and suddenly I could smell the sea. My heart lurched and I felt sick. The pine resin smell vanished and now I could smell seaweed.

'There's a great little beach down this way,' Hannu said, and on he went.

I felt my teeth start chattering. It wasn't the cold. It was me. No way was I going to go one step further. I'd explored the island enough. Hannu turned round, waiting for me to catch up, but I shook my head and looked down.

'You want to head back, Niilo?'

I nodded.

'Sure,' he said. 'We can come to the beach another time. I just wanted to show you the island.' I was looking down at my red Converse shoes – I didn't want Hannu to see I was scared of the sea – and I bit my lip to stop my teeth chattering. He drew up alongside me. 'We're lucky in Finland. We've got thousands of islands.' He kept talking as we walked back through the woods and past the field. 'It's just a shame we don't have lots of wild animals on this island.' He laughed. 'That would be good for a Wild School, eh? If there were elk, bear, wolf, reindeer.' We disturbed a barnacle goose and it waddled off. 'We've only got wild geese, a few hens, two goats and a dog.'

And wild boys, I wanted to say, but didn't.

'Then come summer we might get pestered with a few mosquitoes.' I frowned at that but Hannu just smiled. 'It's okay, Niilo, they're not too bad. They're not fond of the sea breeze. They're far worse by the lakes and in the forests.'

There was a little hill to the side of the Wild School building. Hannu and I climbed this hill. From the top he counted thirteen other small islands. 'Lots of people have got their own island,' he said. 'Behind the ones we can see there are others. And beyond them even more.'

We stood there, gazing out at these rocks in the blue

water. I wanted my own island too, with no one telling me what to do. I wasn't so scared of the sea at this distance – it looked okay, mesmerising even, all blue and shimmery. I just didn't want to go in it.

'Right, Niilo,' Hannu suddenly said. 'We'd better head back.' He didn't want the other staff worrying, he told me.

The other boys didn't exist for me. They were a blur.

Except one. That boy had a scar down his cheek and other scars criss-crossing the backs of his arms. I was in the corridor – escorted, of course – on my way to the library when I first clocked him. I was allowed one book a day. Usually I took books with pictures of reindeer, bears and wolves, and I was thinking about wolves when I saw the boy strutting towards me. He was heading straight for me, so one of us would have to step out of the way. Normally I never did. It was one of my rules – don't move aside. But he wasn't going to stop. And he was taller than me, and there was something about the way he moved, like he'd kill you if you annoyed him. So I stepped to the side.

He stopped and looked straight at me. I'd never seen anyone so scary. His scar looked like it came from a knife, his jaw was hard like steel, and his eyes were like black bullets. 'Hi,' he said, then he was gone.

I swung round but he had vanished. 'That was Riku,' Hannu said. How come I'd never seen him before? I felt a shiver of excitement. So there were two of us here? Two

26

hunters. Two who knew how to turn invisible? Did Riku have the north in him too? I turned back and ignored Hannu, like I didn't care who the boy was.

The rest of the boys were a pack that kept together. Sometimes they screamed. Sometimes they shouted. Sometimes they lashed out. There was one in a room near me who cried for his mum in the middle of the night. They were crazy. And they weren't real for me. I could look through them. Sometimes when I passed with Hannu – in the corridor, or classrooms, or library – I heard them whisper, 'His name's Niilo. He's got one-to-one. He doesn't speak.' I narrowed my eyes and shot them the cold stare.

One-to-one. I liked that. It was like it became my number: 121. I imagined that number on the door of a silver capsule, and in my capsule I had the whole island to myself. I let the chickens stay though, because I liked the clucking noises they made. The dog could stay too because I like that it barked in the night. And sometimes when I hung about in the field, watching Hannu work, the scruffy dog came right up and nuzzled my leg. I wasn't sure about the goats, but maybe Hannu could stay. Or visit.

Maybe the boy with the scar on his face could visit too. Riku.

Maybe.

Chapter Five

After a month at the Wild School I had leafed through loads of wildlife books, watched four films, stared at the sea, edged closer and closer, grabbed pocketfuls of soil, zoomed off in my capsule, got ten letters from my mum that I never bothered to reply to, trotted off on a few of Hannu's island explorations – though never that close to the beach again – and watched Hannu working.

That was about it: a month in the life of Niilo, Wild School prisoner. I felt like a coiled-up spring, like I was getting ready for something, some really big adventure, but I didn't know what. I could feel this wild hunger that Hannu talked about. It was gnawing away inside me. It was hunger for adventure, not for pizza, or chocolate, or cinnamon buns.

Sometimes Hannu came out with weird stories that I half listened to. He said how he had a vivid imagination, and how he always had his nose in a book. Said I should try reading stories too. What did he think? That I was an idiot? That I didn't know how to read? That I just looked at the pictures?

'Once there was a seal,' he said one day, 'that looked like your average common seal but not when the moon was full.' He was placing pebbles along the border of a flower bed and I was watching him. 'You see, moonlight can do strange things to creatures. It can bring the magic out of them. I need a really small pebble.' I thought that was part of the story, but Hannu got up and fished a tear-shaped stone out of the bucket of pebbles. I wanted him to get on with the story, but he took his little pebble and placed it thoughtfully, like he was an artist. 'You see, come full moon, this seal slid onto the beach and what happened was this.' He took another pebble from the bucket. 'The seal skin slipped off and underneath the seal was a man. He jumped up. He ran around. He looked human. All the full-moon night he stayed on the beach, then, full of longing to go back to his home in the sea, he put on his seal skin and slid back under the waves.' Hannu stood up and examined his pebbles. 'Looks good, eh?'

I shrugged. I was imagining a seal swimming under the sea with a human body underneath . . .

I did a lot of standing around, and hardly ever took my hands out of my pockets. Until the day my trousers came back from the laundry and – I'm surprised they took so long – the pockets had gone! They'd been cut out and the slits sewn together. I thought it was quite funny, but I didn't know what to do with my hands after that. They kind of dangled, itching for fat wallets to swipe, euros to filch, cigarettes to hold, ash to flick. I stared at my hands. These were *skilled* hands, and they had nothing to do.

Six weeks in, and it was getting on for midsummer – early June now, with blue skies that hardly ever turned dark. Hannu's seeds that he had planted were coming up, which was kind of magical, and I spent a lot of time just watching stuff grow. We were in our usual spot in the garden when Hannu grabbed my hand and put it up against his own.

'I just read a story,' he said, 'except it's not a story. It's true.' I tried to pull my hand free but it was useless – Hannu was strong. 'It said how, on an island somewhere, they uncovered a burial ground. This burial ground was five thousand years old. That's old, huh? And there were these two hands, skeletons of hands, kind of stuck together, like this.' He moved our two clamped-together hands into my eyeline. 'Imagine, they'd been buried together, and they'd been holding hands for five thousand years.'

'So?'

'So . . .' Hannu carried on as though no earthquake had just happened. But it had! That tiny 'so' was a big deal – it was my first word in six weeks. But Hannu didn't make a meal of it. 'You're probably thinking it's two life-long friends, these hands, or maybe a husband and wife, maybe a mother and son, or twins, but it wasn't.' Hannu kept hold of my hand and I stopped trying to pull it away.

'It was a human and a seal. They had been buried together. Their hands were very similar, like they were related.' Then he let my hand go. 'Quite something, huh?'

Hannu went back to thinning his carrots or whatever he was doing and I dropped my hand by my side. It felt warm. And I couldn't get the image of the man and the seal out of my mind. Hannu liked seals, I knew that.

'I'd like to be that close to a wild animal,' he was saying as he worked. Then he sat up and looked round at me. 'Wouldn't you like that too, Niilo?'

I shrugged. Hannu patted the soil around his little carrots, then stopped and looked up at me 'What is it you really want, Niilo?'

'Freedom,' I muttered, my voice all raw and husky.

Hannu stared at me. Maybe he didn't hear me. 'What?'

I said it again. 'Like the film,' I whispered. My throat hurt. Words tasted strange.

But Hannu got it. He laughed. 'Oh right, you mean that film we watched the day you got here? Yes, sure, I get that.'

I shrugged and looked down. I bit my lip so hard I tasted blood.

Hannu punched the air, just like the guy in the film. Then he brought his hand up against his chest and looked straight at me. 'Freedom's in here, Niilo. We think it's something far away, but it's not. It's right inside us.'

Chapter Six

It was almost a month after the first island rambling, as Hannu called our island explorations. He said we might find some early blueberries now, if we were lucky. Over by the beach.

But I knew he was lying. He thought it was time to show me the beach. He wanted me to trust the sea. 'There's no getting away from the sea on this island,' he said as we wound our way through the birch wood. 'You are brave,' he added, pep-talking me. 'I can see it in your cheekbones.' We were crossing a rope bridge that hung over a small black pool when he said this. That's when he swung round and did that look-right-into-me stare. The rope bridge wobbled. 'We both have something Sami about us, something Laplandish. You must have noticed, surely?'

I shook my head. Sami were the folk way up north who used to run after the reindeer and they mostly had dark hair, like Hannu. I had never thought of it before, but I was sure my parents weren't Sami. My dad was very blond, in fact.

We were still standing on the rope bridge, with it swinging slightly. 'Look, Niilo,' Hannu said, bending his head over the rope and staring down to the pool below. 'Look at our reflections.'

I did, and I got a shock, seeing Hannu and me in the black pool, our reflections gazing up at us, as clear as a mirror. We looked like a painting, two round faces in the water. I looked okay too. I looked like somebody strong.

'It feels like another lifetime, but that's where I'm from. I have Sami blood,' Hannu was saying. 'So maybe it takes one to know one.'

We did look kind of similar. But then a fish or something ruffled the water and our reflections crinkled. Hannu carried on crossing the rope bridge. I could have stayed staring at me in the pool for ages, but I followed him. I jumped off the bridge and followed him through the wood.

'You're from Helsinki,' Hannu suddenly said, 'aren't you?'

'I'm from another planet,' I said and pulled my alien face.

Hannu laughed. 'But maybe you have an ancestor from Lapland? That can explain things.'

'Explain what things?' I leant against a pine tree, looking at him suspiciously.

'Wild nature, and how normal school didn't fit you. I

read your report. What you got up to before you came here. It was like you were a hunter in the middle of a city. It was the wolf and deer you actually wanted to hunt, not wallets. And I've got a name for that – I spoke about it before, do you remember? Wild hunger.'

I shrugged. Outside I kept my face expressionless but inside my mind was whirring. So they *knew*? My parents *knew* about the stealing? So this Wild School was really a kind of prison for people who are too young to go to jail? I looked across at Hannu. Or maybe he was guessing? Could this man see right inside me?

'Sometimes, Niilo,' he said, 'we get lost and do one thing when in truth we want to do something else. I'm talking about substitutes.'

What did he mean? That I hunted wallets when really I wanted to hunt bears? I pictured myself with a spear in my hand, silent-footed, going after a brown bear. A pine cone fell out of the tree.

Then Hannu patted me gently on the back, all friendly-like. 'It happens to people like us. We lose our story. The first time I saw you I knew – you need to find your story.' Then he smiled. 'Come on, Niilo,' he said, 'let's face the fear, eh?'

So he'd guessed. Not for the first time it struck me that Hannu was a bit of a mind-reader. I followed him through the pine wood, feeling weirdly stronger after his little talk about me being a wild hunter with some distant ancestors coming from Lapland. *They* weren't afraid of the sea. They fished the sea. They broke the ice. If that's what he meant by a story, then it was a story I liked.

It was there before I knew it – the sea. I stood at the edge of the small sandy beach and Hannu stood next to me. Suddenly he bent down and scooped up a stone and flung it into the sea. 'Your turn,' he said.

I found a big grey stone and threw it. It felt good to throw a stone into the monster sea. Then he scooped up another one. There was a white buoy bobbing around, probably to say *don't swim past here*, or something.

'Try and hit it,' Hannu said.

So I did, or I tried to. It felt good to stand there, so close to this thing that had terrified me for so long, and fling stones. Then I hit the buoy.

'Bravo, Niilo,' Hannu shouted, and I felt so fired up I could have gone into the sea right then. I wouldn't drown. I wanted to feel the cold water swirl about my ankles. Like my recently invented Lapland mysterious ancestors, I wanted to wade out into the ocean and hunt. Of course, I didn't – but I knew I could have.

It was when we were tramping back to the Wild School building that Hannu suddenly blurted out, 'I won't be here for ever.'

I felt like someone had punched me in the gut. 'Neither will I,' I said. Then I hurried ahead. I was hungry. It was Thursday. We got pizza on a Thursday. If I got back too late there would be none left.

Chapter Seven

That night the nightmare came back: the huge rolling waves, towering like mountains and looming down on me, the screaming, the hands reaching and then the silence. But I didn't wake up like I usually did, heart kicking and this horrible panicky feeling clutching round my throat like strangling hands. Because suddenly the nightmare changed. I was swimming in the sea, and I wasn't scared. The sea was blue and shimmering, not stormy and grey. I was following a black seal, and when I looked at my hand it turned into a flipper.

When I woke I still remembered the dream, and I didn't feel scared. In the early morning light I looked at my hand. I turned it around, stroked the back of it and shuddered – it felt like it was covered in seal skin.

In the garden I wanted Hannu to tell me the story again. He was busy turning the compost that day but all the time I wanted him to tell me the story. It took a while before I could bring myself to ask for it – I couldn't ask him that day, or the next, or the one after. And while I was working up to ask him, I hardly noticed that I had started to do little jobs. I held the bucket while Hannu milked the goats – the white stuff squirted out and smelled rank, and when he asked if I wanted to have a go I screwed up my face and shook my head. But I didn't mind doing stuff like mulching old leaves and turning over smelly compost with a spade.

As the long light days of summer stretched out we moved on to picking strawberries. I liked strawberries. I ate more than I picked, but it felt good to do something. Every night my mouth was stained bright red.

It was on our lunch break, on a long berry-picking day nearly a week after the dream that I finally came out with it. 'That seal and man story?' I said. 'How did it go? I forgot.'

And like before, when I had said my first word, Hannu didn't bat an eyelid, even though this was the first time I had asked him for something. 'Yeah, that was a good one, wasn't it?' he said. 'I thought you'd like that, somehow.' He chewed his rye bread slowly, throwing crumbs for the birds. Then Hannu told about the island where 5000 years ago a human and a seal had been buried holding hands. When he finished he stretched out his arms, indicating the size of the Wild School island. 'I think the island I'm talking about was maybe bigger than this one.'

I was staring out to sea, thinking about seals and hands. I was definitely getting braver, I knew. I'd been working on it – I could look at the sea now without breaking into a sweat. Maybe it was something to do with being so close to it, day and night. Apart from that one time flinging stones, I hadn't been right down to the water's edge, but from a distance me and the sea were doing okay. I watched the cruise ships. I watched tiny yachts on the horizon. I watched the scattered islands. I listened to the sea at night. It was always there, like a giant creature breathing, out and in, out and in. It wasn't a monster any more, just a huge mystery. The water was choppy and white crests broke on the waves.

'Can you swim, Niilo?' Hannu asked.

I shrugged my shoulders. Not really. Anyway, I'd rather be tossed into a cave with a wild starving bear than swim in the sea. But of course I wasn't going to admit to that. I had been taken to swimming lessons in the days when Mum still took me to things, and I remember being bundled up in plastic armbands and kicking about in the pool like a mad turtle. It had felt *good* – like I was at home in the water. But Mum used to sit on an orange plastic chair at the poolside with her hands over her eyes, scared. She said the place gave her a headache.

'No problem,' said Hannu. 'I'll teach you. Sunday.' He picked a strawberry and handed it to me. 'Something tells me you'll swim like a fish.'

Chapter Eight

Swim like a fish? When Hannu said that I glared at him, imagining those staring dead eyes lined up on the fish stalls in the market. Gross. Why would anybody want to swim like a fish? But he was smiling, and nodding and trying to make me feel all positive. I could hardly swim at all, never mind like a fish. All those piano lessons, skiing classes, hip hop dancing and even yoga, all in aid of the 'let's make Niilo normal' project, but after three swimming lessons Mum had given up.

It was the one thing I had thought I might be okay at. The swimming teacher said I showed promise. But Mum said she didn't trust him. She didn't like the smell of chlorine, and she didn't trust the lifeguards. So we stopped. Everybody in Finland can swim, except me.

Hard enough to live in this country and steer clear of the sea, but my parents seemed to manage. On those pointless little summer trips away we always travelled inland. 'I like trees,' Mum would say. 'I like all different kinds of trees. The sea now, that's dangerous. It's for fish.' She chattered away, as Dad drove, like she was terrified of silence. 'We'll all have fun together, won't we? In a cabin in the forest. It'll be so peaceful, and fun.'

Fun? Maybe I just never got 'fun'. Maybe her fear had passed to me, but pretty soon I hadn't liked the sea either. Or trees. And the drowning nightmare didn't help.

So as soon as Hannu brought up the swimming question I felt jittery. I didn't want to look like a total idiot, so I practised on the floor of my bedroom, pushing my arms out and kicking my legs back. What a nutcase. If I wasn't so het up about the whole thing it would have been quite funny, me down on the floor wriggling about like a beached turtle! I tried to remember my three swimming lessons from when I was about five. And I tried to remember the athletes swimming on TV. So I did what they did. Without the water part. Then when we were outside I forced myself to look at the sea for ages and imagine somehow I'd float on the top of it. In my capsule I went swimming in the sea, and it was a breeze.

So, come Sunday, when I realised he meant the teensy swimming pool in the basement I felt let down. And a bit relieved. I wasn't scared of the swimming pool – especially one not much bigger than a wallet. I took one look at it and dived in.

'Hey! That's what you call a belly flop!'

'You do better then,' I shouted, spluttering up water and shaking my wet head. I'd flung myself into the shallow end and practically hit my head on the bottom but I didn't let on. It was just like a bath, a big bath, and I wanted to put my training into practice, so I took off, thrashing up the pool.

Hannu ran and dived gracefully in, even though there was a sign up saying 'no running'. The sign said no to lots of things, but Hannu seemed to ignore it. He came up beside me where I was kicking around in the water and trying to grab the rail at the side. 'Grab these instead,' Hannu said, flinging me a pair of armbands. I didn't want armbands – I wanted to do it on my own – but then I started to go under so I reached out and grabbed his hands.

Hannu led me away from the side of the pool. 'See,' he said, 'I knew you'd be a natural.'

'How come?' I yelled, kicking my legs all over the place and trying to keep my head out of the water. 'I haven't done anything.'

'Exactly,' said Hannu, swimming backwards and guiding me round the pool. He didn't mention the armbands again. 'You didn't drown. You took one look at the water and you were in it. I was going to suggest the steps at the side of the pool, but no, you just dived right in.'

'I thought we were going to swim in the sea. This is for babies. Like, I did this ages ago.'

'How about you close your eyes for a moment. I'll lead you round and you try and imagine the sound of the sea. You know, the waves lapping up against the rocks. Above you, the gulls are screaming in the blue sky.' As he spoke Hannu swam backwards, pulling me round the pool.

'I don't like gulls. They steal your food.'

'Not these gulls, Niilo. They watch over you, making sure you're okay. Some people say the gulls are the souls of drowned sailors.'

'That's rubbish.' I kicked out my heels, splashing water up onto the poolside, but I still kept a tight grasp of Hannu's hands. 'Total garbage.'

Hannu laughed. 'Might be. Might not be. And what about the mermaids? Those beauties with the long golden hair, eh? You know, Niilo, there are a lot of wonderful, magical things in the sea. I love the sea, though it scares me too. Like when it's stormy.'

'You're crazy.'

'Okay, so mermaids and magic and the like, they're just stories. But remember how some stories are true? And hey, I knew it, you're a born swimmer. The way you're kicking your legs back? That's brilliant – like a frog. So how about we try the story where I let you go and you push forward with your arms, in big wide strokes. Like you're swimming free in the ocean.'

'What if I go under?'

'I'll bring you up again.'

'What if I don't want to do this stuff?'

'There are plenty of logs out there needing to be stacked into piles.'

I grinned. It had happened a few times lately and the

sensation was strange – it didn't feel like my face, twisting into this shape – but I couldn't help it. Hannu grinned back and gently uncurled his fingers, setting me free. I kicked back with my feet and reached out with my arms, as though I was trying to grab at the water but couldn't get hold of it.

I started sinking and I cried out. I swallowed water. Then I went right under. I grabbed onto Hannu and he lifted me to the surface, choking and spluttering, and brought me right up onto the poolside. 'That was brilliant, Niilo,' he said.

I spat out the water. 'It was rubbish,' I said. 'And I'm not a frog. I don't want to be a frog.'

'Okay. You're a seal. So, want to try again?' He nodded towards the orange armbands at the side of the pool. 'With a bit of plastic help?'

I looked at the water, and shrugged. 'Okay, but if anybody else comes along I'm taking them off.'

So for half an hour, Hannu and me – unsinkable with the armbands – swam round and round and round. 'Stupid of me to let your hands go,' Hannu said, looking really upset. 'You have to get used to being in the water. It's a different world. What was I thinking? Maybe I was too full of the old stories. I was too pushy. I'm sorry, Niilo. You looked like a natural.' He was swimming alongside me, telling me to kick and glide and stuff like that.

'That's okay,' I said, and we kept going, round and round and round. Sometimes Hannu swam backwards, coaching me. And sometimes it did feel like the sea, with the waves lapping against the rocks, and the gulls in the blue sky overhead circling and crying. And I wasn't scared. And I knew Hannu was right. I *was* a natural. It was like my legs and arms knew about water. I knew how to swim. Okay, I had armbands, but even though I had this help, I felt strong.

'You heard of Ahtola?' Hannu said as we made slow circuits of the pool.

'Who's that?'

'Not who. What. It is Finland's magical land under the waves. Where mythical sea creatures live. They make the waves, they care for the tides and the fish – there's a whole kingdom down there. All kinds of creatures live in Ahtola, like Vellamo the sea maiden, or so the stories go, but most of us don't see them. And there's old Vainamoinen, the father of Finland – they say his mother gave birth to him in the sea. You know, Niilo, there's more magic around than we might think. The magic ones keep the seas clean by chanting spells. They feed the good folk of Finland.'

'What about the bad folk?'

Hannu laughed. 'I wouldn't know about them. Seems to me the ones we call bad are sometimes the best, but they just don't know it yet.' He pulled over to the side of the pool and looked at me hard. '*You're* not bad, Niilo. That's a story you tell yourself.'

'You're a rubbish storyteller, Hannu,' I said, and kicked back my heels. Hannu swam after me. We circled the pool in silence, and somewhere, way down in my memory, I did remember that I had heard stories of Ahtola. Maybe these old stories were from way back, before I built my capsule and lived in it. Or perhaps it had been the only thing I'd listened to in school.

The teacher's voice had droned on through the dark afternoon. '*Vainamoinen, old and steadfast . . .*' I was listening, but pretending I wasn't. I was looking out of the window at the sky over Helsinki, growing dark, but there was something about the rhythm of the teacher's voice, and his tale of this father figure, with his long beard and huge muscles, born out of the air maiden in the sea, chanting magical runes and looking after the people of Finland. The teacher's voice murmured on and it was like I was back there. '*Then did Vainamoinen, rising, set his feet upon the surface of a sea-encircled island, in a region bare of forest . . . there he dwelt while years passed over, and his dwelling he established, on the silent, voiceless island, in a barren, treeless country.*'

I felt a shiver shoot up my spine as I remembered this. I liked stories. And this one told of a magical place that had nothing to do with houses and schools and cars and stuff. There was a world under the waves, and it was like my capsule – a safe and magic place. There, mermaids lived and creatures could change shape. There, a woman changed into a salmon.

I wasn't scared of the sea of Ahtola.

'Poor old Vainamoinen. He never did get himself a wife.'

Hannu's words cut in on the memory and water rushed into my mouth. I spluttered and yelled. I had been imagining the blue sky was above, not the ceiling of the swimming pool. 'Easy does it, Niilo. Hey, you're okay,' he said as I grabbed his arm. 'You did well. You swallowed a bit of water. Nothing to worry about. You looked like you were out there on the ocean. Maybe someday you will be.' Hannu guided me to the poolside. 'That's our time up. Let's get dressed.'

'Tomorrow?' I said, climbing out of the pool, water dripping from me. I yanked off the armbands. 'Can we do it tomorrow? Can we go to the sea tomorrow?' I was still scared, but more in a thrilling way. It was like the fear had shifted into excitement with a hint of danger.

'Steady on, Niilo. It takes time. You need to work up confidence in the pool first. You can't swim yet, don't forget that.'

'So, okay, I'll come here tomorrow. I'll learn fast. And anyway, I practically can swim. I want to come again tomorrow.'

'I don't know,' Hannu said. 'We were lucky to get a free slot today.'

He must have seen the disappointment sit back over my face. That is so typical, I thought. Something goes well, then something else comes along to spoil it . . .

We went into the changing room and that's when I saw the red slash mark down his back. I could see stitch marks, loads of them – Scarface was nothing compared with this.

I swallowed hard, wondering what had happened to him, but I didn't ask. We dressed in silence. Hannu threw the damp towels into the wash basket and looked round at me, but I looked away.

'If you would join in with the other boys you could come here every evening, you know.'

I punched at the wooden bench and ignored Hannu. 'They do a swim hour seven till eight every night. I heard it's lots of fun.'

I spat on the tiles.

Hannu shrugged, then checked the timetable on the wall. 'Looks like there's a free space on Tuesday, Niilo,' he said. 'I'm off on Tuesdays but Tomi works then. He'd be happy to take you swimming.'

I scowled and shook my head.

Hannu sighed. 'Well, if you insist on always doing things on your own, then you'll have to wait for the same time next week.' He sounded irritated.

I glared at him. 'That's stupid,' I shouted. 'That's ages away. What do you have to be off for? I'm not off. You go off this prison island and I never do. You play in a band and I don't.' I ran for the door. 'It's all rubbish.' Of course, the door was locked. I kicked it. Hannu followed me over there, but took his time. He brought the key from his pocket, opened the door and escorted me back to my room. He didn't say a word. We walked in silence, apart from me banging my fist against the wall and stomping my feet on the wooden floorboards.

'I play in a band because I spent ages practising the guitar.' We were near my room when he said this. He said it slowly, like he was getting annoyed with me. 'If we want to become good at something we need to dedicate ourselves to practising.' Then he snatched in a deep breath. 'Like I said before, you have a skill in picking things. You could probably pick the strings of a guitar. You want to play guitar?'

I shrugged. I was still cut up about the swimming stuff, and the rules. I wanted to *swim*. Now he was going on about guitar. Then suddenly I had this image of me doing a drum solo in a rock band. Maybe Hannu was a mind-reader.

'Or some other instrument maybe? Keyboards? Drums?'

'Maybe drums,' I muttered.

'There's a music studio in the school,' he said. By this time we were at the door of my room, but I still didn't look at him. And I couldn't believe how bad I was feeling about the swimming thing. I'd got myself so worked up for swimming, and now he was wittering on about music. 'I can see about getting you music lessons, if you like. Maybe we can fix that up for you.'

'I thought we were going to swim. I want to swim. You're confusing me.'

'Sorry,' he said. 'We're supposed to offer you variety. You know, bit of this, bit of that. That's part of the philosophy – widen your horizons and all that. Give you opportunities.'

'I don't want bits of this and that.' I glared at him. 'I

want to swim in the sea.' I couldn't believe I was actually saying that, but when the words came out I knew it was true. *That* was what I wanted. He could stuff his guitar or his drum kit, and his dedication. I wanted to get off this island. And learning to swim in the sea would be a first step to swimming to freedom. Maybe I could make it all the way back to Helsinki, or find my own island, or sneak onto a boat? I wasn't only skilled in picking things. I could be skilled in swimming, I knew I could.

'I'll see what I can do,' he said, cutting in on my escape plans. Hannu sounded none too hopeful.

'Whatever,' I mumbled, then yanked back the door handle and snuck into my room.

'Goodnight then, Niilo,' Hannu said.

I slammed the door in his face. But I didn't hear his footsteps go off as I stood at the other side of the door. I could feel he was still there, at the other side. We stood like that for ages, then I heard him tap the door.

'Listen, Niilo,' he said, his voice kind of choked up. 'There's something I have to tell you. It's not about swimming, or music. It's about me . . . moving on.' I didn't say a word. 'I told you already I won't be here for ever.' There was a long silence. 'Are you listening, Niilo?'

I didn't move. For all he knew I could have been under the bed with my head under the pillow, so I blanked his words. I thought he was going to come clean about his huge scar, or witter on about playing in a band, but Hannu didn't tell me anything.

'Niilo?' he tried.

I still didn't move. I hardly breathed. He didn't say anything after that, and after about ten minutes I heard his footsteps go off.

Chapter Nine

When I saw Hannu the next day he didn't mention the thing he had to tell me. 'You know,' he said, when we were in the workshop together, pulling the green tops from the strawberries and tossing the red berries into a huge copper pan for jam making. 'That smile suits you, Niilo. It's like the sun has come out.'

'I've been practising,' I said. I felt in a good mood – I don't know why, I just did.

'What? Smiling?'

I laughed. 'No! Swimming. I've been lying on the floor, doing the strokes like you said. I think I could swim in the sea. If I wanted I could escape from this prison.'

'You want that?'

'Freedom,' I said, as though that word said all the other words I couldn't.

Hannu had these dark eyes that saw right into you. 'Like I said, Niilo,' he said, giving me the serious look, 'it's in there.' He pointed to my chest, meaning 'heart', I suppose.

'Easy for you to say.' I pointed my finger at him now. 'You knock off at six. You jump on that ferry. You take days off. You zoom about on your motorbike. You listen to music. You play in a band. You go into bars. You smoke . . .'

'I don't smoke.'

'Well, you could. You do whatever you feel like. Easy for you to say freedom's in here.' I whacked my chest hard.

'Whoa, steady on.' I saw a shadow flit over his face. Maybe he freaked at how hard I'd hit myself. I was going to do it again, so he grabbed my arm. 'Look, Niilo, I know you're angry. That's okay. But don't beat yourself up.' He let my arm go and I let my arms flop. 'You and I need to sit down and have a chat. There's something I need to tell you. I tried—'

But I interrupted. Whatever Hannu needed to tell me, something told me I didn't want to hear it. Something deep inside. 'I could find old man Vainamoinen,' I blurted out. 'I'll find Ahtola, and I'll escape from this hole. I'll do what I want. Vainamoinen can be my dad. Then I'll find my seal skin and put it on. Then, whooo, off I go, under the waves.'

Hannu smiled. Maybe he forgot whatever it was he was going to tell me. 'Hey!' he said. 'So you like my stories, huh? Thought you said they were rubbish too, like the island.'

I shrugged and shoved a huge strawberry into my mouth. Then I suddenly lunged at Hannu as though I was going to punch him. Hannu drew back, then laughed as I did, but I knew I'd scared him. 'Or maybe,' I said, doing a funny dance around the table, 'I'll find pirates and live with them. Sail the seven seas and all that. That's the kind of life I want. Always going places. Never hanging around. Nobody telling you what to do.'

'And wearing a black patch over your eye?' Hannu winked at me. 'Drifting with the tides. Drinking rum, and pretty girls in every port. That's the life.' He pulled the top from a strawberry and lifted the bright red berry into the air. 'My girlfriend likes these . . .' His voice trailed off and he started whistling a pop song.

I stopped my daft pirate jig, letting the strawberry that was in my hand fall back onto the huge chopping board. 'You look too old for girlfriends.'

'Hey, I'm only thirty-three. That's not old.' Hannu shook his black hair back and jutted out his chin, like he was showing me how young and handsome he was, but I saw worry flash through his dark eyes and I saw how he bit his lip. 'I thought I'd mentioned her before. Actually, Niilo, we're getting married soon. That's part of—'

'Nice.' I stared at him, hardening my eyes, dropping the smile. 'Probably I wasn't listening. Probably you did mention her, and I didn't care.' I threw a strawberry into the pot.

'Listen to me, Niilo. I'll be leaving soon. My girlfriend has a job further north so I'll be going away from here. I need you to know that, Niilo. And you're doing really well.'

I shrugged like I didn't care what he was saying. And we worked at these blood-red strawberries for ages. We cut the berries up but it was the air between us you could have chopped.

Suddenly Hannu blurted out, 'Saara.'

I frowned, like I didn't know what he was talking about.

'That's her name.' Hannu sounded apologetic. 'I mean, my girlfriend. She's called Saara, and she likes strawberries. We'll have one of these strawberry chocolate-fountain things at the wedding. You could come along, maybe? My band will be playing. Not me, though. I mean, you couldn't exactly play at your own wedding, eh? They'll have to find another bass player.'

I made like I wasn't listening. But inside me the big black hole had come in again and I was sinking down into it fast. Hannu was going away. He was the only teacher in this place who bothered about me and he was getting off this prison island, like everybody else did – except me.

Hannu said nothing more about weddings and the two of us worked in silence, throwing strawberries into the huge pot, pouring in sugar, stirring the sugar into the berries, then turning the gas ring on and hoisting the heavy pan over to the cooker. There was comfort in having something to get on with, but the silence between us was awkward. I knew I was over-reacting – why shouldn't Hannu have a life? – but I couldn't help it. I tried to drum some sense into my brain, but it wasn't working. I felt as though I had crawled into my capsule and sailed off a thousand miles.

Hannu chewed his lip. Sometimes he looked at me, but I always looked away fast. Twice, he cleared his throat, as though he was getting ready to speak, but the words died in his throat. When finally he did speak, all he said was, 'So, Niilo, you going to stir this jam or just stare at it?'

I dunked my wooden spoon in the huge copper pot and mashed the sugar and strawberries together, harder than I needed to. The red juice splatted out of the skins like bright blood.

'Hey, Niilo,' Hannu said, 'I have good news.'

I kept jabbing into the strawberries.

'We'll have strawberry jam for supper.'

'Big deal.'

'And I got more.' Hannu sounded excited. 'Yeah, wait for it, Niilo. This is really good news.' He cleared his throat and I knew he was waiting for me to look round at him. When I didn't, Hannu carried on, 'Yeah, seriously good news. The boss says, now it's warmer, and now you are showing an interest in swimming, I can take you swimming in the sea!'

I said nothing for a while, but stopped bashing the strawberries. I swallowed hard and felt my heartbeat race. The sea. The thing I hated most was the thing that would take me to freedom. I pushed down the panic that was rising from my gut. I was tough. I was hard. And, whatever it took, I was going to show Hannu that I could swim in the sea. I nodded my head and stared into the red mush. 'Cool,' I mumbled.

'Yeah,' Hannu said. 'I thought you'd like it. You have to wear a buoyancy aid to keep you afloat. That's the rules. But if you're okay with that we can go tomorrow. Management say you're doing well.'

The jam started bubbling. 'Cool,' I said again. 'That's cool.' I would look like a dork with a rubber ring round my waist, but for once I didn't care.

Chapter Ten

The clock on the wall crept. It was two a.m., then half-past three, then quarter to four. At five I got up and dressed. I sat on the edge of my bed, waiting for Hannu. I couldn't stand the feeling of hoping so much. What if Hannu didn't come? What if a storm came and we couldn't go into the sea? I'd psyched myself up so much that I had to face this fear.

I, Niilo, was going to swim in the sea!

What if Hannu woke up with a headache? Or the staff ferryboat didn't run? If anything happened to ruin this trip I was sure the disappointment would kill me. Hannu wasn't due until nine a.m. and I was expected to eat bread and cheese before that, in the mad dining room. Hannu had talked me into doing that with one of his stories about folk doing cool stuff together and having fun. Like you could too, he said, in the dining room. You could meet friends there. Then he said how Riku always went to the dining room, and that had swung it for me. So I'd been trooping in with the rest of the bad boys for a few days now. Then, after breakfast, I was even expected to help clear the breakfast dishes. What if I dropped a dish? What if I lost my temper?

I survived breakfast, but I could hardly eat today. Every time the door opened I swung round. 'You waiting for your sweetheart?' one of the older boys said, sneering. I so wanted to punch him in the face, but dug my fist into my other hand and gripped it tight. They just didn't get it. From across the table Scarface looked at me and chewed noisily, like he was curious how I would react.

'Cut it out,' the staff member said.

'Coz Hannu's already got a sweetheart,' the boy whispered, 'and it ain't you.' Then he tittered like a fool.

'I said, cut it out.'

A hush ran round the dining room and I made like I hadn't heard him. I bit into the bread. Nothing was going to spoil this day. Nothing.

'They're jealous,' Riku said, coming over and sitting down next to me – I got the feeling he was protecting me. He tore off chunks of bread with his teeth like he was a wolf. We both chewed noisily. 'You're gonna swim in the sea?' he said, eyeing me sideways.

I nodded, my mouth crammed with bread. I swallowed it down. 'How do you know?' I asked him.

He didn't answer that, just winked at me and tore into another chunk of bread. 'You gonna escape?'

I shrugged and tore into the bread, same way as him. 'Might do.'

'Somebody else tried that,' he said, looking straight ahead. 'Last thing he ever tried.'

I choked on the bread. 'Did he drown?'

'Heart attack, they said.' Then he swung round and stared right at me so I was close up to his scar – it looked like he'd got himself into a seriously bad fight and I wondered what had happened to the other guy. 'It's cold out there,' he whispered, spy-style. 'If you're gonna make it, you need grease.'

'Grease?'

'Yeah. Grease. Lots of it.' Then Riku got up and swaggered across the dining room. At the door he stopped and glanced back at me. He winked and was gone.

When Hannu finally arrived that morning I punched the air. I was in the canteen wiping down the tables and the boy who had taunted me at breakfast now laughed out loud. Hannu strode over to me before I thumped this guy, and steered me out of the canteen and into the corridor.

'Ready for the sea?' he said, all cheery. 'Because I am.' He had a light grip on my arm and led me out of the building. By the time we were outside, under the hot sun and clear sky, I had forgotten I was angry. I swung round. Through gaps in trees I spied the massive blue sea and for a second I felt my knees buckle. I reached out and grabbed at Hannu's arm. I was shaking.

'Whoa, boy,' he said, steadying me. 'We don't have to do this. We could do something else. Gardening?'

I shook my head, but I still felt sick. Scenes from my nightmare flashed into my head and I had goose bumps prickling my whole body, but I so wanted to go into the sea. Maybe I really was crazy.

'Well, if you're sure,' Hannu said. 'It'll be cold, remember. I know it's July, but even so the sea is still pretty chilly. It'll feel much colder than the heated swimming pool.' We made our way down the path that led away from the school building and skirted the fields where Hannu's lettuce and carrots and stuff were shooting up. 'The sea's not like the swimming pool,' he added.

'Obviously,' I said, trying to act cool.

'I mean, water's about all they have in common. Seriously, Niilo, you'll probably get a big shock when you first go in, but then you'll get used to it. I can't believe you've never been in the sea. This is going to be a big deal for you.'

I wished he wouldn't go on about it. I could hardly speak, I was that nervous. Hannu had a bag slung over his shoulder and I spied the orange life-preserver sticking out.

'Yeah,' he went on as the sea, between tall pine trees, got closer, and bigger. 'Apart from the cold, there's the waves. Not that the Baltic is big on waves, but there's pulls and currents. You'll feel it.' He stopped by a wooden bench, slumped the bag down and rummaged in it. 'Here,' he said, pulling out my life-saver in fluorescent orange. 'You wear that round your waist and you'll be unsinkable.' I felt like a kid holding a rubber ring and I swung round to check nobody was watching. 'Relax,' Hannu said, probably reading my thoughts. 'They're all in the study room this morning. It's just you, me and the sea.'

We followed the nature trail that led past the gardens with all the fruit bushes. Hannu made a detour so we could feast on a few raspberries, then say hi to the goats. When we were at the goats I asked him. 'Is it freezing? I mean, could I get a heart attack?'

Hannu patted the goat and shook his head. 'We're only going to stay in the bay. It'll feel a bit chilly, but not freezing.' Then he looked up at me, knitting his eyebrows together. 'You heard the story of the boy who died?'

I nodded and chewed my lip.

Hannu stroked the white goat again before we headed off across the island. 'It was before my time here,' he said as we walked, 'but I heard he had a weak heart, and got into trouble in the sea. Poor guy.' Hannu took a deep breath. 'Look, Niilo. We don't have to . . .'

'I want to.' I was going to say something about grease, but it felt like a giveaway, so I left it at that.

'Okay then, buddy, let's go!'

We tramped over the heather. It was a small island so it only took us about ten minutes to skirt the pine forest, hike over the heather and reach the sloping rocks that led down to the sea. Face to face with the huge flat and glistening water, I felt a shiver shoot up my spine . . . So, this was it. The monster. Mum's horror stories came flooding back. Every sinking ship. Every drowned sailor. Every oil spill. Every freak wave. Every shark attack flitted across my mind. I was panting, and I hadn't even swum a stroke yet.

'You okay, Niilo?'

I nodded, clenched my fists and pushed all her horror stories away. 'Sure I'm okay.'

We stood watching the water. The sunlight glimmered on the sea's surface like a million dancing coins and it looked dazzling. 'It's pretty polluted, you know,' Hannu said, breaking the silence. It sounded as if he was apologising for the sea.

'So your mermaids better chant more spells,' I said.

Hannu nodded, but he looked like maybe he didn't believe in all his stories after all. 'Yeah, you're right about that.' Then he pulled off his T-shirt. 'I mean, it will be fine to swim in, but it's not clean like it used to be.' He kicked off his flip-flops. He had his shorts on, ready to swim, and he took a couple of steps down to the water's edge and let the water run over his feet.

I was behind him and could see that scar on his back again. It looked like he'd survived a sword attack, and it gave me courage, thinking that if he could survive that, I could survive swimming in the sea.

'When I was a kid,' Hannu was saying, 'the water was clear.' Then he turned his head round to smile encouragingly at me. I was still on the beach, clutching my rubber ring and gaping wide-eyed at the sea. 'So I'm told, anyway. Thing is, I don't remember too much about being a kid.' He stopped smiling. 'I never told you, did I? I lost my memory.'

'What are you on about?'

Hannu shrugged. 'Nothing. Okay, let's swim! Come on, Niilo. A few steps and you're in.'

Maybe that's what he'd been trying to tell me? Maybe I'm not the only freak around here. It made me feel stronger somehow, so I yanked off my sweatshirt and wriggled into the stupid orange float. The sea made a low roaring noise and, high in the air, a gull screamed. I kicked my trainers off and took my first step into the sea.

Hannu was right by my side. 'Okay so far?'

I nodded. The water swirled around my ankles. The sudden cold gave me a shock and my legs felt like jelly, but I took another step over the rock and sunk deeper into the water. Every horror-filled thought that screamed in my head I batted away. Hannu was right next to me as we waded in, deeper and deeper, and the cold water snaked around my legs. I was tough, I was strong, I told myself. I looked down and my legs were vanishing, being eaten up by sea. I gasped, but I was getting used to the cold. And Hannu was right – it wasn't *that* cold. I felt gritty sand ooze between my toes and forced myself to take another step, then another.

'So you tell me you were never in the sea before?' Hannu

stopped when we were waist-deep. 'That's quite something.' He flicked water up onto his chest, and looked like he was getting ready to flick water my way, but didn't.

'My mum was scared. Said she hated the sea.' I could feel my voice trembling.

'Something bad happen to her?'

I shrugged. I didn't want to think about her. Not here. This was a huge deal for me. I just wanted to think about swimming in the sea. I took another step and the water level rose to my armpits. The rubber ring bounced up – my body was going under, but this orange ring wouldn't. 'Don't you worry 'bout a t'ing,' Hannu sang in a reggae voice. He splashed water over his face. 'Trust me. Nothing bad's going to happen to you, Niilo. We're not going to go deep. We're just going to stay in this shallow little bay. Bend your knees, push forward with your arms like we did in the pool, and that float will look after you just fine. And I am right here next to you when you need me. You ready?'

I nodded, bent my knees and was getting ready to push forward when I suddenly stood up and said, 'What do you mean, you lost your memory?' I knew I was stalling, but I wanted to know.

'I'll tell you all about it some other time.' Then Hannu pushed forward. I watched him swim three, four strokes, then he twisted round in the water like he was a seal and swam back. He stretched out his hands. 'Swim towards me,' he shouted. 'You can do it!'

I forgot I was frightened. It was like, now that I was

finally in the thing I was terrified of, I wasn't terrified any more. Or maybe it was Hannu, being Mr Super-Encouragement, that made the fear go away. Whatever it was I felt fine. I pushed forward, kicked my legs back, and swam.

'Great!' Hannu yelled. He was swimming backwards and I was thrashing through the sea like a mad thing, trying to grasp his hands. The float did its job, though – it wouldn't let me sink. I laughed and slapped my arms down, making spray shoot up into the air. 'Let's make for that rock out there,' Hannu shouted. 'I'll swim right beside you. And if you panic just shout and I'll be right there, okay?'

'Okay,' I shouted, water running into my mouth. I spluttered and thrashed my arms.

'Whoa!' Hannu said, lifting my chin out of the water.

I stopped coughing and laughed. I felt terrified and excited at the same time.

'That's it,' Hannu said. 'Keep your head out of the water, and kick back those legs. We'll drink some water when we get back. You don't want to drink this stuff. Okay, Niilo, let's *swim*.'

I pushed forward with my arms. I could do it. Okay, the rubber ring helped, but it was me swimming.

'Yeah,' Hannu yelled, 'that's fantastic!'

And when I got the hang of it, I didn't want to stop. I couldn't believe it – I didn't feel scared at all. I swam further and further, kicking my legs, thrashing through the water, pushing forward with my arms in big wide strokes like I had practised on the floor. I was doing it. I was swimming! And most of all, I was in the sea!

'This is way better than that baby pool,' I yelled. All the time Hannu shouted encouragement. I kept my head well up, I kicked back hard, I flung my arms forward, I panted and gasped and the Wild School island grew smaller behind us. We reached the rock and hauled ourselves up onto it. I felt as though I'd swum for Finland. My skin tingled. My muscles ached. I had done it! I couldn't keep a huge grin off my face. 'That was great,' I cried out, panting hard. 'That was the best thing ever.'

'You did just brilliant,' Hannu said, looking out to sea. Out of nowhere a speedboat roared past, bumping up and down on the surface.

'Wow! That's pretty cool,' I yelled.

Hannu said nothing.

We sat for a while on the rock. It was only thirty metres or so from the shore but for the first time in over two months I was off the island. It was like I suddenly saw it, this island that had become my prison and my home. I watched it, this strange school that was nothing like school. I watched the fir trees, the birch trees, the sloping rocks. I knew that behind the ring of trees lay the garden and the strawberry fields. And beyond the garden was the school building, with the boys in the study room, and the swimming pool in the basement, and the canteen, and the chill-out rooms and the games room and studios and the offices and the corridor, and off that long corridor was my little room. It all felt miles away.

'I had the feeling you'd do it,' Hannu suddenly said.

'Do what?'

'Swim.'

I laughed again. I had never felt this happy – not that I could remember anyway. I had done it! It didn't matter that the float had helped – I had swum in the sea! I stood up on the tiny rock and punched the air and the rubber ring fell to my feet. I was stronger than the nightmare. 'I did it!' I yelled, and lifted both arms high into the air. Like the guy in the film I'd seen on my first night at the school, I punched my fist into the air. 'Freedom!' I shouted, and Hannu clapped and cheered, like I was some kind of superstar.

Chapter Eleven

Those next few days, full of sky, sun and sea, were the best days ever. It was a hot summer and I felt like I was on holiday. Hannu was given the go-ahead to teach me to swim better too – that's what he told me. He kept trying to bring up the topic of his leaving, like he was preparing me, but I didn't want to hear. I zoned out when he went on about it. I just wanted to swim.

And Hannu was right – I did swim like a seal. The Wild School, Hannu kept saying, believed in giving their pupils space, and time. 'They want the best for you,' he kept telling me. I didn't care what the Wild School wanted. *I* wanted to swim in the sea. And I wanted to swim further and further out. After three days, I left the orange baby float on the rocks, waded straight into the Baltic – and swam. On my own! Hannu said he wished work could always be like this. 'This is the life, isn't it, Niilo?' Hannu, swimming on his back, splashed up water with his feet.

I did the same, swimming as easily on my back as on

my front. 'Think I could swim to Sweden,' I shouted, flicking a spray of water over Hannu. We were swimming way past the white buoy and I overtook him, then flipped over and yelled, 'You trying to help me escape?'

Hannu dived deep and rose up through the water next to me. 'That's exactly what I'm trying to do. But not in the way you think.'

We swam on. By now the Wild School island was half a kilometre at our backs. The vast horizon lay shimmering ahead.

'You don't get it, Niilo,' Hannu said as we swam, slowly now. 'I told you. Freedom's an inside thing.'

I kicked my feet back hard and felt a fist of anger surge through me. It was so easy for him to prattle on about freedom being an inside-yourself thing. What rubbish. 'Try saying that when you hear your bedroom door click locked behind you at night.' I treaded water and ranted, 'Try saying that when you get no phone, no cigarettes, no Xbox, no nothing except boring old books from the library. Try saying that when you have to stay in the school and watch all the staff go off home on the ferry. Try saying that when you can't choose what to do. Try saying that—'

'Okay, Niilo. Okay. I'm sorry.'

I swam away fast and dipped my head under so Hannu wouldn't see what was tears and what was sea water.

He switched to front crawl to keep up. 'Niilo, I said I'm sorry. I'm just trying to do the right thing, that's all.'

I swam without saying anything for a while, then

suddenly turned to him. 'What do you mean – you lost your memory?'

We swam slowly. I could feel him dragging his story up, getting it ready for telling. I didn't look at him – sometimes it's easier like that. We were swimming further out to sea when he told me: how he'd had a car crash when he was twenty-three. He'd just left Lapland, where he lived. 'I was heading south to Helsinki – to the big city. I'd bought my first car. I was so proud of that car. There was ice on the road. Black ice. And I was probably driving too fast. The car skidded. That's the last thing I remembered.' Hannu told me how he had been in a coma for four months, and when he came out of it he was fit and healthy, apart from the slash down his back where the edge of the car door had wedged into him . . . but he couldn't remember a thing. If it wasn't for his father, he said, sitting by his bedside with photo albums and telling him stories of his childhood, he wouldn't know who he had been.

We were still swimming, slowly. The sea was glassy and warm. 'Bits come back to me,' Hannu said. 'Sometimes I think I can remember, then I think what I remember are the stories my dad told me. Most of my memories now are made up from old photographs. But you see, Niilo, he gave me my story. I had lost it. It's like I lost myself, and he gave me back to myself.' He gave me that funny look again, like he was thinking of me and my lost story. 'Anyway, we better head back now. Race you to the rock.'

He took off and I swam after him. But I couldn't stop

thinking of Hannu losing his memory. And black ice on the road to Helsinki. Of the car he was so proud of, skidding. Swerving out of control. Of his dad telling him who he was.

Who was I? That's what I wanted to know. Or maybe I didn't. I thrashed my legs, forgot about everything and pushed forward through the water with all my might. Maybe Hannu slowed down deliberately, but we touched the craggy rock at the same moment. I was panting and gasping like mad. 'I won!' I shouted.

'It was a draw,' Hannu said, hoisting himself up to sit on a flat patch of rock. I saw the way he watched me clamber up after him and I swallowed hard. In the past I would have insisted I'd won. I might have grabbed the nearest thing and thrown it. I would have made a major fuss. On this rock in the sea there was nothing to throw. The car door had wedged into his back . . . I couldn't get that image out of my head. Hannu kept staring at me, and I chewed my lip and pulled at my hair. Then I hoisted myself up and plonked myself down beside him.

'Okay,' I agreed, 'it was a draw.' I let my breathing slow down. 'That's one impressive scar,' I said.

Hannu nodded. 'I suppose so. I forget it's there most of the time. I put it behind me.' He laughed, like he had just made a joke. It wasn't that funny, but I laughed too.

When the laughter died away we sat on that rock out at sea, saying nothing. Gulls wheeled above. I watched the Wild School island. From the rock it was just a huddle of

71

pine and birch trees and the top of a red-brick building. Beyond that island I could see bumps in the sea. Those were more of the jewels Hannu talked about. More of the archipelago. And here and there small yachts glided past.

'I don't get it.' I turned to look at Hannu and frowned. 'Like, I've learnt to swim, and, for God's sake – make jam! I know about nettles, berries, weeding and planting seeds. I can cut the top off a strawberry and know the difference between a pine tree and a birch tree but, seriously, is that it? It's supposed to be a school, isn't it?' I shrugged. 'I mean, I've been here ages.' I flicked my hand towards the island. Drops of sea water spun through the air. 'I thought I was here to learn stuff.'

Hannu nodded. 'I suppose that's the idea.'

'Like, maths and stuff,' I went on when Hannu said nothing.

'Yeah,' Hannu nodded. 'Maths and stuff.' He laughed then, a soft kind of laugh. I laughed too. It all felt like a big joke.

'What is the Wild School anyway, some education experiment in nature for the seriously disturbed?'

'That's one way of putting it.'

'And are my parents actually paying for this? For me to make jam?' I laughed again, suddenly picturing myself going back home with suitcases packed with jars of jam.

Hannu laughed too. 'The government pays most. This kind of education isn't cheap, Niilo. But yes, your dad pays towards it. He said he wanted to help you.'

I couldn't believe that. He wanted *rid* of me, but with the sea all around me, and my muscles feeling alive with all the swimming, I didn't care. 'I keep wondering when the proper lessons are going to start.' I didn't look at Hannu when I said that, I just gazed out to the sea.

'Personally,' Hannu said, 'I think maths is overrated.' He laughed again. 'I find shamanic singing more interesting than maths.' He turned and looked at me. 'Ever heard of it?'

I shrugged. 'Sounds weird.'

'It is. Anyway, I hadn't heard of it,' Hannu went on, 'until about a year ago. I met this man from the north, from Lapland. I've already told you that's where I'm from. Originally, I mean – I've been away a while. And, so my dad told me, I was one of the modern Laplanders, not into Santa Claus and chasing reindeers and stuff. Certainly not into singing and magic. That's why I wanted to go to Helsinki, I guess, to live in the modern world. Anyway, I was lucky. For this job at the Wild School they send you on these expeditions. So there I was, back in Lapland doing this training course. We were often going on hikes in nature. There was a big group of us, but me and this old Laplander usually walked at the same pace. Slow. Maybe it was the car crash did that to me, but I like to go slow now. Anyway, me and him were on a long hike through parts of Lapland – huge lakes, dark forests, bear and elk and reindeer. You should go there if you can, Niilo. It's magical.'

'I'm a prisoner, remember?' I said, but for once it didn't

come out bitterly, more like a joke. I clamped my wrists together, like they were handcuffed.

'Oh, yeah,' Hannu said with a laugh. 'I forgot. Anyway, me and him got talking, and one night we shared smoked salmon and rye bread under the midnight sun. That's when he told me about the shamanic singing. They call it "yoiks", or wild songs. It's a kind of singing. It's like, everything and everyone has their song. But some people don't know their song. Or they lose it. And it isn't only people who need a song. It's animals too. Even trees and stars and everything. So me and this Nils – that was the man's name, a bit like yours – we finished off the bread and then he said: *Hannu, my brother, I give you your wild song!* See, I'd told him my story, of losing my memory. It was like I had lost part of myself. And something told me this Nils was about to give the lost part back to me. Like my dad had done with his stories and photos, only more.'

I didn't say anything. After that big speech Hannu didn't either. He fell quiet, like he was trying to remember his wild song.

'So?' I said finally.

'Well, it was strange. The old culture, they have a different language, so I didn't understand the words. Like I said, after I lost my memory it was like my past vanished. The old man looked at me for ages, then he closed his eyes and next thing he started chanting. It sure wasn't your average pop song. But when he sang in this strange voice I could feel his song putting me together.' Hannu gazed out to sea, like he was remembering it all, way up there in the far north. Then he looked at me. 'It felt as though I had been kind of broken before.'

'Sounds pretty weird,' I said. Except it didn't. Not deep down. People could get broken, and random stuff like songs could put them together again.

'It *was* weird. But in my bones I understood it, and in my heart. Maybe this sounds mad to you, Niilo, but it was magical. Because afterwards, after he had chanted this song, all the time in this strange language, and sometimes making movements with his arms, I felt better. A whole lot better. Better than I'd felt for years. I was pretty lost, you know. Yes, my dad had helped. Sure he helped. But there were still missing bits. A kind of emptiness. The wild song filled that.' Hannu paused, like he was hearing that strange wild song again. 'And it wasn't long after that trip I met Saara.'

Next thing he was going to tell me when he was leaving. I had heard enough. I stood up, gripped my toes over the jutting edge of the rock and jumped into the sea.

'Before the trip to Lapland I was so afraid of getting close to someone.' Hannu was standing on the rock, shouting. 'Do you know what that means, Niilo?'

I heard him, but I didn't turn round. I kept swimming back to the island. Hannu dived in after me. In the distance the bell in the main school building rang for lunch time and I was already dressed and running through the woods by the time Hannu waded ashore. He pounded after me.

I glanced back and saw him, his T-shirt flapping out in the breeze, his flip-flops in his other hand.

Halfway along the nature trail he caught up with me. He flung his T-shirt on the ground, grasped me by the shoulder and swung me round. 'I don't tell everyone what I just told you. Listen to me, Niilo. I told you because I had this feeling, when you get out of here, head north. Find your wild song. You and me, Niilo, we have the north in our blood. I told you that already. And you're not bad. You've just lost your story. And your song. We're similar, you and me. We've been brought together for a reason. And like I say, I won't be always here.'

I broke away and ran on, through the garden and into the courtyard of the school.

Hannu caught up with me again. 'Niilo, listen.' He tugged at the sleeve of my shirt. 'There's something I need to tell you. About me leaving . . .'

Just then a swarm of boys spilled out after a gym class. The courtyard, that moments earlier had been empty and silent, was now a hub of noise and chatter. One of the older boys saw us and wolf-whistled. I tugged away from Hannu and slipped into the building.

In moments I had shut myself in my room. Whatever he wanted to tell me, I didn't want to hear it. I slumped down on my bed with my hands over my ears. I had this sudden memory of Mum and all the times she had been trying to tell me something, and I had never wanted to hear.

Chapter Twelve

Five minutes later Hannu was knocking at my door. 'Niilo,' he called, 'it's me. It's Hannu.' He knocked again. 'What was that sudden disappearance about? That was important stuff I was telling you. We were doing so well. You swam fantastically in the sea. Niilo?'

I pressed my ear against the door, but I didn't speak. Then I heard footsteps, heavy footsteps. 'Leave him, Hannu.' It was Stubble, the head teacher. I knew his voice. 'You know by now what our boys are like. They need time in their cave.'

Next thing, I heard footsteps growing faint. They were leaving. I gave them a few seconds, then opened my door and stepped out into the corridor. My door wasn't locked during the day and I closed it without a sound. I could see the head teacher sweeping Hannu along, so I used my skill and crept behind them, keeping in the shadows and not making a sound.

'And you understand, don't you?' the head teacher went

on. By this time they had reached his office. They were standing at the door of the office. I slunk right in against the wall. 'In this line of work it doesn't do to get too close. Yes, you've done wonders for poor Niilo. I think you've really made a breakthrough. He looks less miserable, that's for sure. And he even smiles now. He's like a different boy. That's great. Being outdoors has really helped. And being able to swim will give him a sense of achievement. But while you're still here we'd like you to concentrate on the older boys. We're changing your timetable.' Then Stubble disappeared into the staffroom, leaving Hannu standing in the hallway.

At the other end of the long corridor I pressed my back against the wall. Just then the bell rang for supper and a swarm of boys filled the corridors. One of them snuck his arm in under my arm. I didn't know who it was. But he pulled me away, pretty much the way Stubble had swept Hannu along. Normally the other boys left me alone, but now here was one tall, stupid-looking guy, acting like we were the best of chums. I tried to pull my arm away, but whoever had a hold of me was strong. 'It's Samuel's birthday,' this guy said, still pulling me along. 'You want cake, don't you? And there's going to be ice cream.'

I frantically looked round for Hannu, but he was gone. Next moment we were in the canteen. It was bright and noisy. The boy gripping me steered me up to a table, already crowded with boys, and plumped me down on a bench then slipped in next to me.

I had special one-to-one treatment. Apart from the crazy breakfast times I didn't even eat with the others. I only ever spoke to Riku – Scarface – and was never so close up to the other boys. Scarface wasn't at this table, and I could feel my heart kick in my ribs. 'Hey, see who I got to come to the party,' this boy was yelling and boasting to the boys around the table. They just stared at me.

We were all considered bad, but I guess, apart from Scarface, I was the worst. I had homemade tattoos and a pierced eyebrow and I think they thought I couldn't speak. I could stare anybody down. I was the one who punched, kicked, spat and doled out the evil eye. I never mingled with the others. I knew no one. I trusted no one. Right now, I hated sitting at the table with these boys squashed all around me, but I wasn't going to show I was scared. Anybody dared look at me and I glared at them. I could see how freaked some of them were. Good. The staff member at the table didn't look too comfortable either.

'Great to have you join us,' the staff member said unconvincingly. 'Isn't it?' he added, looking round at the other boys who too quickly, too eagerly, nodded their heads.

I glowered at them all and said nothing. But the older boy by my side, the one who had grabbed me in the first place, kept it up. I looked around for Riku, but couldn't see him. 'Yeah, really good to have you join us. I mean, you're going to have to put up with us for company now. No special—'

'Jaakko, that's enough,' the staff member cut in. A tremor

of tension ran round the table. 'Right, who's for chicken soup?' he piped up. 'Hey, Niilo, how about you?'

I was starving after all the swimming, but hemmed in like this my appetite had gone. I squirmed on the wooden bench. I had Jaakko on one side and the staff member on the other. The young boy opposite started making clucking sounds and was told to shut up. I pushed my empty bowl away and shook my head. Inside, I was working really hard not to start screaming, stand up, push the table back and run out.

'You sure?' the staff member went on, dangling a soup ladle in the air.

I nodded. There was a basket of crusty bread in front of me so I reached out, grabbed a chunk of bread and bit into it. A zing of tension ran round the table.

'Hey! We haven't started yet,' the clucking boy said. 'We start together. Look at him! Look!'

'It's okay,' the staff member said. 'We'll let it go this time. Niilo doesn't know how we do things. We haven't had the pleasure of his company much.'

'Will soon.' Jaakko grinned.

I crammed the bread into my mouth, my brain working feverishly. What did this Jaakko fool mean? I was going to have to put up with them for company now? It pounded in my head like a war drum. What on earth did he *mean*?

'Soup, Jaakko?' the staff member asked, a bright strain to his voice. I swallowed the chunk of bread and grabbed another piece.

'Yeah, sure, I'll have chicken soup.' Jaakko flashed a look round at me and his nostrils flared. His blue eyes had that shine of triumph about them, or madness. With my mouth crammed with bread I gripped my hands into tight fists under the table and watched the man next to me dish out soup. It slopped into Jaakko's bowl and looked like puke. The staff member pushed the bowl in front of me. I felt sick. I shook my head, then pushed the bowl away and brown liquid sloshed over the rim and onto the table-cloth.

'Hey, you're messing the table up,' the clucking boy said. 'I don't like mess. I hate mess. Mess really gets me upset.'

'Chickens died for us,' another boy said, and giggled. The boy clucked again. The staff member told him again to be quiet. He was counting to five. Voices flew back and forth, and the voices grew louder.

The staff member reached five. He got more and more anxious-looking. His eyes flickered around the room, like he was expecting someone with more authority than he had to save the day. No one came. His face flushed red. 'That's enough,' he said, first under his breath, then louder. 'That is enough!' Nobody took any notice.

'I can't s-s-stand mess,' the boy stammered. 'I mean, it does s-serious stuff to me. Mess.'

Jaakko, who seemed to be the gang leader, pulled at his soup bowl and clattered his spoon on the table. 'Ooops! Sorreeeee,' he said, looking around the whole canteen and grinning. There were eight or nine dining tables and it looked like they all had their own dramas going on, but our table was centre stage. The prima donnas of the dinner time. The serious nutcases! The ones everybody was looking at. The noise of the canteen racketed in my brain like screeching gulls.

There was a lull in the noise. That's when Jaakko sighed. 'Jesus, it's too bad,' he said. Everyone around the table looked at him expectantly. He waited, like an actor milking the pause. 'Big shame Hannu's leaving so soon.'

'Leave it out, Jaakko,' the staff member snapped.

'What?' That was the first word I spoke. A knot tightened in my gut. 'What did you say?' Of course I knew – Hannu had been telling me for ages – but I had never truly believed it.

A silence fell over the whole table. Spoons dribbled brown chicken soup. The staff member beckoned to a colleague across the room, and two burly men came over. The next few seconds happened like a slow-motion action scene in a movie.

'Hannu is leaving,' the staff member said stiffly, getting to his feet. 'He's getting married next month, then they're going north to live.' He nodded to the man who had come to stand by his side. He looked back at me. 'He told you. He said you knew, Niilo.'

I felt the smooth table edge in my hands. I gripped it tight – then *pushed* it. Bowls, spoons, bread, glasses of water, napkins, salt cellars, even the small vase of flowers in the middle of the table rolled slowly downwards. It was like a keeling boat. Soup spilled onto boys' laps. They screamed. The table leg reared in front of my face.

The three men had a hold of me in a second. One pinned my arms back and others lifted me into the air, as if I was a doll. With my feet off the ground I watched the table crash to the ground and everyone fall down, or stagger to their feet – all in slow motion. A napkin floated in the air. The boy who hated mess howled as the table slammed down on his legs. Another boy punched the boy next to him and the whole dining room erupted like a bar-room brawl. I watched the scene of chaos as I was carried out. It was as if I was watching a film. None of it was real. I was outside of it, looking in and watching, and none of it was real.

Just before they carried me out of the canteen I saw him: Scarface. He was leaning against the wall, sucking juice out of an orange, the only one not fighting. He looked at me, and winked.

Later I sat gazing out of the window in the nurse's room. I could see the branches of an oak tree, and on a branch a squirrel was feasting on an acorn. That squirrel was free to go where it liked. Sunlight spilled through the branches of the tree, lighting up its red bushy tail. If I could just concentrate on the squirrel, everything would be all right . . .

Behind me, people came in and out. The door creaked open and shut. A spoon tinkled in a coffee cup. Murmured voices spoke about what to do. Hannu burst into the room. Still I didn't turn around.

'I am sorry,' Hannu said. He was right behind me. Still I sat and stared at the squirrel. 'I did tell you, Niilo, several times,' he went on. 'I got the feeling you weren't listening. But I never made it a secret. I'm leaving, Niilo. And it doesn't matter. This is about you, not me. And you're doing well.'

The squirrel turned the acorn around in its paws, gnawing away and swishing its bushy tail back and forth.

'He'll be fine in a day or two,' the nurse at her desk piped up, sounding none too pleased with Hannu. 'He's had a bit of a shock. This is the Wild School. It happens. You should leave now.'

Hannu ignored her and moved round to stand in front of me. I watched the scene like it had nothing to do with me. 'Look at me, Niilo,' Hannu said. 'For God's sake, *look* at me.'

I moved my head to the side so that I could see the squirrel. It was still there. The acorn was getting smaller.

'Well, if you won't look, at least listen.'

I put my hands over my ears. The squirrel dropped the acorn and scurried up the branch. I could still hear Hannu.

'I worked hard with you. And I did that because I wanted to. Not because it was my job. And we've done well, Niilo. You've made great steps. Strokes too!' He laughed then, but the laughter quickly faded. 'But Saara, remember, I told you about her. We're getting married, and Saara has a job up north. The wedding is in one month's time. Then

I'll be gone from here. This Wild School job, it was always temporary – I told you that. I know you're finding this hard, but it'll work out fine. You are a good strong person, Niilo. You are going to make it.'

'I am going to insist you go now, Hannu,' the nurse said. She tapped her pen on the desk. 'He's very tired. And I think you are upsetting him again.'

'Yeah, maybe I should go, but right now I'm sick of what I should and shouldn't do.' Hannu glared at the nurse. 'Just give me more time. We know each other well.' He swung back to face me. 'Listen to me, Niilo. We're getting married on the tenth of August and I want you to come to the wedding. It's on the island of Suomenlinna. I've told Saara lots about you. She asked for you to be there too. Come with your family.'

'Really, Hannu, I am going to ask you to leave now. Please!' The nurse stood up and opened the door.

I didn't blink, didn't show any sign of having heard a word, or even having seen Hannu. Of course I'd heard every word, but it didn't mean anything. I went into The Capsule and turned the music up loud.

Hannu squeezed my shoulder then drew back as I stared at my knees, my hands floppy on the chair. He walked to the door, his steps heavy and slow, stopped halfway across the room and looked back. 'I'm here three more weeks.' I could hear the nurse pick up the phone. 'Goodbye then, Niilo,' Hannu said. 'I believe in you, remember that.'

I heard the nurse get up and open the door. I heard Hannu's footsteps move away, heavy and slow. Then the door closed.

When I looked up the squirrel had gone.

Chapter Thirteen

I refused to leave my room for three days. The suicide watch kept an eye on me – not that they called it that, but that's what it was – a boring job for the one who had to come into my room every hour and check I was fine.

Mostly I slept. Then when I wasn't sleeping I lay staring into space, planning my escape. I was a skilled thief. The more I thought about escaping, the more I knew I could pull it off. I knew how to move without a sound. How to dart in and out of crowds and shadowy places. I could make myself invisible. And now I had another skill. I could swim. And not just a few strokes. I knew, if I needed to, I could swim for hours. I was a born swimmer. That's what Hannu had said, and it was true.

The more I slept the more I dreamt. As the days became meaningless the nights became full of images and adventures. And in these dreams I was swimming. I was swimming with seals. I saw hands in my dreams, Hannu's hands, the skeletal bones of a seal's hands, and other hands: hands without arms, hands stretching out to me. In my dreams I reached to grasp these hands, but woke before I touched them.

I lay awake in the middle of the night. I say *night*, but being summer it was light almost all the time and I hardly knew what was day and what was night, but I did know by now how the Wild School operated. They let children lie in their caves – that was the expression they used. They'd give them three or four days, then they'd move in and it would be back to weeding, berry picking, chopping wood, candle dipping, cooking, wood carving, drawing and sitting in circles where I was supposed to talk about my feelings.

It was loneliness that drove me back. The option had been given to me, after three days of solitary, and I grabbed it. Loneliness, and a vague plan. I couldn't escape if I was lying in my room all the time. I needed to have a good look around. I needed to check out possible exit routes. And I wanted to see how Hannu was managing without me. So I shuffled along the corridor.

'Good to have you with us,' a new staff member said. 'I'm Bernt and you and I are going to be great friends.' I didn't think so. 'We've got circus skills this evening. Most of the boys here really enjoy circus skills.' His voice was annoying me.

'What's that?' I grunted. 'Lion-taming?'

Bernt laughed. 'Stilts and juggling,' he said. 'Fun stuff like that.' Whoopee! How old did he think I was? Five?

It didn't look to me that evening like most of the boys

88

enjoyed it. Most of them were playing the fool, making stupid faces and falling off the stilts. Bernt was busy trying to get me to join in.

'It's part of it,' he said. 'Getting the clown inside you to come out and play.' I was doing my usual disinterested leaning back against the wall thing. We were in the games hall and there were four corners of stuff going on: the stilts, juggling balls, tightrope walking and putting a red nose on and looking silly. It was noisy and I couldn't believe how useless they all were. They fell off the stilts, dropped the balls and wobbled about, then jumped off the tightrope, screaming. I flashed my eyes about, looking for Hannu. 'Have a go,' said Bernt.

I shook my head. Then I saw him. He was the only one not wobbling about on the tightrope. He was in charge of a group of boys and they were all gazing up at him, like he was a king – I hated them. Hannu was walking the tightrope with his arms out to the side. Sometimes he stopped. He had this serious concentration look on his face, not that he would hurt himself if he fell since the tightrope was only about one metre off the ground, and even then there was a soft landing mattress thing underneath. I willed him to lift his eyes and look at me, but he didn't. He reached the end of the rope and the boys cheered.

Bernt was still at my elbow. 'Try the stilts, Niilo. You can start with a low pair. It's easy – you just have to remember to swing your arm and leg at the same time.

Left arm and left leg together. Right arm and right leg together.'

So I did. I knew I'd be good at it and I wanted Hannu to see how good I was.

'Slow down, Niilo,' Bernt called out, worried. He had been standing beside me when I took off. After ten seconds I was halfway down the hall. 'Niilo, come back!'

I stilted fast. I wove through the jugglers. I snap-snapped these wooden stilts all the way to the tightrope corner.

'Check *him*,' one of Hannu's boys said, whistling. 'He's pretty ace.'

I did a fast twirl, like I was stilt dancing.

'Showoff,' another one said.

'Hannu's not working with you any more,' somebody else chanted.

I couldn't see Hannu. Where was he? I heard one of the boys sneer and I broke then. I jumped off the stilts, flung one of them at Sneering Boy and swung the other one above my head, like it was a lasso. That changed their tune. Sneering Boy was screaming while I was looking for the one who had called me a showoff. They were all screaming now. Running for the door. Then I saw Hannu.

'Niilo,' he said. He stepped towards me, but stopped at the distance of the swinging stilt. His face was a map of hurt. 'Stop it, Niilo,' he said. 'Put it down.'

The stilt was whipping through the air. It whirred. I was going to hurl it, but Hannu stepped forward, shot his hand up and grabbed hold of the stilt. Then he looked straight at me. He was trying to say sorry with his eyes. I spat at his feet, let the stilt go and swung round.

I slammed right into Bernt.

I couldn't get the image of Hannu's hurt eyes out of my mind as Bernt escorted me back to my room. 'So you lasted thirty-five minutes out of this room,' he said, checking his watch. 'We'll talk this through in the morning, when you've calmed down. And you'll apologise to Tore. We don't tolerate violence, Niilo.' He folded his arms and leant against the door, watching while I sunk onto my bed and kicked my trainers off. 'Like I said, Niilo, you don't know what you're missing. There's good stuff goes on at this school. If I was you I'd shape up and get involved. Think about it, okay?' I heard the key turn in the lock, heard the staff member's footsteps stride off, growing fainter and fainter. Then it grew awfully quiet in the corridor.

I kicked at the door till my toes ached. I pressed my forehead up against the door and stood like that for a long time. The sounds from outside grew quiet until I guessed it was lights out. No footsteps went by in the hallway. From along the hallway another boy yelled. A door slammed. Then it was quiet. I felt a cold prickle of fear and banged at my door.

'Hannu!' I shouted. 'Hannuuuuuu!' I heard my voice fade into nothing. Again and again I shouted, till my throat hurt. It was only when I banged the door hard with both hands, like I was drumming round some primal camp fire, that I heard footsteps approach. I stopped hitting the door.

A river of sweat ran down my spine and my heart jolted. 'Hannu?' Whoever was outside had stopped at my door. 'Is that you, Hannu?'

'It's bedtime, Niilo,' came a voice that wasn't Hannu's, from the other side of the door. It wasn't Bernt either. Maybe it was the janitor, or the night-watchman?

'Get Hannu,' I said, pressing my face against the locked door. 'Tell him he's got to come.'

'He's not coming, Niilo. Now get some sleep. It's late.'

But whoever it was didn't move away, and it felt comforting somehow to have somebody, some anonymous somebody, talk to me from the other side of the door. I slumped to the floor, exhausted. The man at the other side of the door was still there, unless he had slipped off his boots and slunk off in his socks? The thought hit me with a cold panic. I knocked at the door.

'You still there?'

'I'm still here, Niilo.'

'Don't go . . . will . . . you.' My voice was breaking. I didn't care. I was past cool. Past tough. Past bad.

'I can't stay here all night,' the man said, his voice hushed though it was loud enough to be heard through the closed door. 'Go on, get some sleep. I'll wait here ten minutes if that's going to help you.'

My face was pressed up against the door. 'You could sing me a lullaby,' I said, then laughed. I couldn't believe I had said that. What a baby! 'Just joking.'

'Trust me, you don't want to hear that,' the man said,

then laughed too. A couple of minutes passed. He coughed. Then he said, 'You in bed yet?'

'Yeah,' I lied, still slumped down behind the door. 'Just sinking into dreamland . . .'

'Good, because I gotta go.' This time he really walked away. I heard his footsteps snap, snap down the corridor, fading into nothing.

Maybe I did dream, there on the cold floor. Because when I woke, stiff and freezing in the middle of the night, I knew what I had to do. I had to be 'good'. If I could hold it together and show that I was, as they liked to say, worthy of trust, I would find a way to escape. They were always droning on about trust in the Wild School. 'Trust us and we trust you' was one of the mottos. Okay, I would be so good they'd trust me with knives and matches.

Hiking on the island and practising what the staff called 'survival skills' was popular. I climbed into bed and felt a glimmer of hope for the first time in days. Here was a plan that could work. It might take one or two weeks, so I would need to be patient, but all I needed to do was to play it their way, or pretend to. Then, acting like the model pupil, I would slip away undetected, wade into the sea and swim for freedom.

The Baltic was littered with islands. I wouldn't have to swim far, an hour, maybe two. I could do that, no bother, I was a natural. Then I'd have my pick of islands. It suddenly seemed so easy. I lay my head down on the pillow that felt like cotton wool after the wooden floor, and worked it all out. I'd seen the film *Castaway*. And Hannu had told me about Robinson Crusoe who had lived on a deserted island. I felt my pulse race. I would disappear, being Mr Good Guy, and swim to freedom. I would have my own island. Other people had done it. So could I. And there were plenty of empty summerhouses I could break into. I'd be my own person, with no one telling me what to do and what not to do. Once I was free my life would fall into place. Things would work out. It wouldn't always be like this. I wouldn't always feel so useless. So rubbish.

Suddenly, lying there in the dim summer's night, I had this image of myself strong and happy. But happy wasn't going to happen in a locked room. Happy wasn't going to happen on this island with its rules and rye bread, and Hannu gone. Happy would happen when I was free.

I would need to be super-fit. I would need to work up stamina. And take books out of the library about foraging in the wild. And I would need to keep my cool. I would master those breathing exercises. And all that relaxation, feel-great-about-yourself stuff they went on about in the Wild School. I would do it all. I would even do that meditation stuff. I would be the master of cool control.

I sat up straight. I started right away. I closed my eyes and counted to ten, then I repeated the words, *I am strong. I am peaceful.* I repeated them ten times. Then I opened my eyes. My training had begun!

The next morning, early, I turned up in the canteen for breakfast. The boys drew back and looked at me. Their chatter died and an uneasy silence ran round the room, till Bernt jumped to his feet and pulled back a chair for me. I felt like a celebrity rock star, returning after a world tour. 'Good morning, Niilo,' he said. 'Porridge?'

'Sure,' I said, even though I hate the stuff. Then I added, after a short pause and a strained smile, 'Thanks.'

It was pretty boring being good. I had to apologise to Sneering Boy, who had a sore leg. I had to fix up one of the stilts that I had broken. I kept having to remind myself that I was good. Every time somebody asked me to do something, everything in me wanted to say no, but I forced myself to say yes. They kept praising me like I was some baby who had just learnt to walk. Every little thing I did they went all gaga.

I peeled potatoes and they patted me on the back.

I pulled up lettuces and they kept telling me what a great guy I was.

I sat quiet in the library while some hippy told us a story. It wasn't about Ahtola. It was about some mouse that was greedy then got caught in a trap. Another mouse helped him out and after that the greedy mouse started sharing everything with the one that helped him. The stories were so obvious it made me want to spew up. But I didn't. I sat there with a glazed expression on my face. So great that you're joining in, the storyteller said, beaming at me.

Sometimes I caught Riku staring at me, like he was

wondering if I'd joined the other side. I didn't know if I should tell him my plan. What if he blew it? We were on the same team setting tables in the canteen one morning when he came up to me. 'I got some,' he said, banging down a plate.

I put the knife and fork beside it. 'Some what?'

'Grease.' Then he scanned the room, saw nobody was watching us, whipped out a jar that he had stuffed down his top and pushed it towards me. I grabbed it and stuffed it down my hoodie. 'You got to cover yourself with it. It'll save you.'

I wanted to ask him why he didn't escape too. I wanted to ask him why he was helping me. But some teachers came into the room and started sorting chairs. 'Nice table setting,' one of the teachers said. They were praising me for everything. I plastered on that false smile, twirled a fork in the air and said, 'Hey, thanks.'

I never saw Hannu. I kept looking for him, but maybe he had already gone.

Chapter Fourteen

'It's really great to have you join in, Niilo,' Aleksi, the team leader said. I was part of a team now. We were called 'the Eagles', and we were berry picking. Aleksi wasn't the real team leader – he was filling in while the usual team leader was on holiday – and he wasn't as trained up as the other staff. I could tell that. 'Hannu was right about you. He said how he believed in you, how you just needed time, and care.' Aleksi laughed and nudged me with his elbow. Staff weren't supposed to nudge you with their elbows. I knew that. Staff weren't supposed to talk about other staff either. I knew that too. 'That's the way men who are getting married talk, eh, Niilo? They go all soft-hearted.'

Aleksi was seriously annoying me. 'I filled my basket with berries,' I said. 'What am I supposed to do now?'

'Wow, Niilo, slow down. You'll leave none for the other boys. They're not as fast as you. I think you should just relax in the sun for a bit, then you could help Kari with his picking. You've been working so hard lately. Take a break.'

'I don't need to relax.'

'Gee, I wish you would. You make me nervous, fidgeting and tapping your foot constantly. Look, Niilo, you did good work. And when we do good work, we get rewarded with little breaks. That's what I'm giving you. A little break.' Aleksi laughed, but not in the warm and open way that Hannu had laughed. This was more of an aren't-I-the-funny-man laugh. It made me sick, but I kept a smile tugging my lips up. It was getting harder and harder. And Scarface had started to frown at me, like I had turned colours. I felt exhausted with it all. I squatted down at the end of the field.

'That doesn't exactly look relaxing,' Aleksi shouted, pointing to my awkward-looking position.

'I'm relaxed,' I said too sharply, then thought I'd better add something nice. 'It's fine, honestly. I like sitting like this. Thanks for being so concerned.'

Aleksi shook his head, looked like he was ready to make another comment, then let it go. He flipped a hand in the direction of the new boy called Kari who had arrived three days before. Kari had his hands in his pockets and he'd already kicked over his basket. 'Hey, Kari!' Aleksi shouted over to him. 'They tell me Niilo here was just like you. Now look at him! Fastest berry-picker in Finland!' Aleksi laughed and sauntered over to where I was hunched down. Lowering his voice he said, 'Kari's finding it really hard.

His parents died in a motorbike crash and he couldn't cope. You can't blame him, poor guy. And it seems his grandparents don't want him.' Aleksi looked back at the new boy. 'Hey, no pressure, Kari,' he called over to the glum-looking boy, digging a hole in the earth with the toe of his boot. 'Don't feel you have to do anything, okay?'

'Wish my parents had died in a crash,' I said. *Nice* had just snapped.

'Jesus!' Aleksi shook his head. 'I can't believe you said that.'

'I said it.'

'Well, forget what I said about relaxing in the sun. Get up and take those strawberries into the kitchen, whip off the stalks and wash any flies off them. Then if we're lucky we'll have strawberries and cream for supper. Hand them over to the cook, then come straight back, okay?'

'Okay,' I mumbled, lifting up the basket of strawberries and trying to think of something really morbid so that the huge smile threatening to break open my face wouldn't give the game away. I had either been locked in my room or under surveillance constantly since I'd arrived on the island, and here was Aleksi telling me to go off 'on my own' and wash the strawberries!

I strolled off, whistling, and resisted the temptation to break into a run. I took the path that followed the nature trail, round by the pine trees. I had Riku's grease with me. It was kind of awkward, stuffed inside my shirt, but ever since he had given it to me I carried it on me, just in case.

Once behind the dark trees I dropped my basket of strawberries. The red berries spilled down onto the grass. Then I ran. I tugged at my shirt, buttons snapping. There was something great about that ripping snapping sound. One tug and the shirt fell to the ground. I held the jar of grease and kicked off my shoes, then paused, thinking I might need them. For a second I stared down at my prized red Converse shoes. They cost a fortune. And they would come in handy. Quickly I tied the laces together and slung them round my neck. I ran on, my shoes bobbing up and down. I ran faster and faster. Only one thing was worth treasuring now: *freedom*.

My heart pounded against my ribs. I couldn't believe this was actually happening. I kept into the shadows and ran barefoot without making a sound. In moments I was down on the sloping rocks by the sea. The sun shimmered on the surface and small waves sang.

'*Come, Niilo, come in.*' That's what they were singing. '*This way freedom. Come!*'

I shot a glance back over my shoulder. No one was coming after me. I unscrewed the jar and started plastering the grease all over me. It felt slimy and weird but I smeared it all over till I was covered. It was like a skin, a seal skin! Then I hurled the empty jar into the bracken, snatched in a deep breath, held my shoes and jumped from the rocks down onto the small sandy beach. One stride, two, three and my feet were in the water. After the shock of cold the sea felt tingling. Warm, even. Maybe it was the grease? I waded further in, trying not to splash up water. I couldn't believe my luck – there wasn't even a boat out to blot the blue horizon.

I waded deeper till water swirled round my waist, then rose up to my shoulders. I glanced over my shoulder. Nobody was coming. A gull swooped low. I fell forward and took the first stroke to freedom. Goodbye Wild School. I swam fast, cutting through the sea with hardly a sound. The shoes slung round my neck got in the way. So I threw them off me. Two red shoes bobbed, then sank. I kicked back my heels. This was it. Escape!

For the first time in a long time the future called like a thrilling adventure. I passed the rock where Hannu first told me about finding his wild song. I swam fast now. Soon I was far out. I wanted to yell, I wanted to kick back water and cheer at the top of my voice. But I kept the yelling locked inside. Further and further out I swam and with every stroke grew stronger. I kept going, slicing my arms through the water. I felt so strong, like I could take on the ocean.

By this time I was farther out than I'd ever been. I was a natural. I swam like a seal. I twisted onto my back and watched the Wild School island shrink. 'Freedom,' I murmured, twisting round and reaching forward through the water. Then I said it louder. Who would hear? No one. I was alone. Me and the wide blue sea. I threw up a spray of water. The word burst from my lungs. 'Freedom!'

Chapter Fifteen

I swam like an Olympian. Further and further I swam. Sometimes I flipped round onto my back and kicked my feet. It gave me a rest, and I liked watching the Wild School island grow smaller and smaller. Then I turned and swam on . . . and on. I felt great. This felt way more exciting than filching wallets, but why did no one come to look for me? Why was there no rescue boat? Could it be my escape hadn't been discovered? Was Aleksi so daft that he'd forgotten I was on his team? Like, how long does it take to wash strawberries?

I spun round and swam on, making for another island. The archipelago was littered with islands, and I saw a few dark dents break the endless blue. Hannu would have said they were all like Finland's dark beautiful jewels, scattered far and wide. I batted thoughts of Hannu away. If Hannu knew I was missing, he'd send out a search party. Probably he'd dive into the sea and swim after me. But the other staff, they didn't care. Probably they would be glad to see the back of me.

I kept swimming. When I felt my muscles ache I floated on my back and gazed up at the blue sky. I couldn't believe how easy this was. Why didn't everybody swim away? What about Scarface? Why didn't he escape? I rolled back onto my front and swam on. And on. I wondered where Hannu had gone? It felt lonely out here. I was a drop in the ocean. But I kept going. I planned not to let up until I couldn't see the Wild School island any more. I glanced back over my shoulder. The island was tiny now, but I could still see it. I wanted to put it behind me. Like Hannu and his scar.

For what felt like hours I swam on, but my arms didn't zip through the water now and my legs didn't kick back so strongly. At least the weather was okay. I watched the sun pass over me in the huge blue sky. Then I saw it slowly slip downwards. I had been swimming all afternoon and I could feel the beginnings of a pain across my chest.

Keep swimming, Niilo, I spoke to myself. I panted hard. *Keep going.*

Every stroke now was a massive effort. My chest felt fit to burst and my arms and legs ached, heavy as lead. And worse than that, the fear was creeping back. It was like it had never gone away, just gone to sleep. Now it was waking up and saying – where the hell are you? Jesus, this is the sea. The *sea*!! Have you any idea what's under you? Skeletons. Sharks. Killer whales. Are you mad? Monsters too. Are you totally insane? And what about the drowning nightmare? What about the waves that any

103

minute now are going to turn into hungry mouths and swallow you?

The fear started small and grew. It grew fast. It sucked my strength away until I could hardly take another stroke. I had to think of Hannu. If I didn't, I'd drown. Or I really would go crazy. I imagined a story Hannu would tell, of how the people of Ahtola would scoop me up into their arms and guide me to safety through the waves. I imagined the wise old Vainamoinen, singing on his kantele and looking, looking, always looking, for a bride. I imagined the beautiful young Aino, pursued by the ancient Vainamoinen. I pictured her long hair flowing, her sandaled feet pounding down as she fled through the woods. I pictured her fleeing into the sea, and changing into a salmon, and leaving old Vainamoinen alone by the edge of the sea. Now she was the angel of the sea. She was looking after me.

That's when I saw the seal. It lifted its sleek black head out of the water, hardly a stone's throw away, and looked at me. I thought I was seeing things, like I had conjured my own magic. I thought I really had gone crazy – I was bringing Hannu's stories to life.

But this creature didn't vanish into thin air. It swam towards me. All the fear that was in me focused on this strange creature heading towards me, on its yellow eyes! I felt terrified, but weirdly calm at the same time. I forgot about sharks and monsters and skeletons. Even the exhaustion vanished. I heard a whimper in my throat. Then the mysterious creature slipped under the water. I waited for it to brush against me, or come up behind me, or right in front of me. It was like some torture game. But then I saw the seal way ahead. It swivelled its head to look at me. And maybe I really was mad, but I got the feeling the seal wanted me to follow it. And the way it looked at me didn't feel scary. And I could see, beyond the seal, a dark shape. There was another island ahead.

I thought maybe I'd been swimming in a big circle and this island ahead was the Wild School island. But I looked over my shoulder and I could still see the Wild School . . . if that dark rock in the distance *was* the Wild School. But there were lots of distant rocks, lots of small islands. I wasn't sure which one was the Wild School. I felt dizzy and I didn't know what was happening.

I was in the sea, and I was following a black seal.

I was escaping.

I was exhausted.

I didn't know where I was going, but I just kept swimming, pushing my arms forwards and pulling the sea back.

Sometimes the seal looked back, like he was checking I was still with him. I didn't know too much about seals, but they weren't scary like sharks, and the pictures of seals in books made them look cute. I didn't even know if this creature was a seal. It could have been a dolphin, or a walrus. Maybe it was one of the creatures from Ahtola? Maybe it was a human with a seal skin on? Maybe I was dead and this was some kind of afterlife?

But the sea felt like water. The sky looked like sky. And I was panting hard. I didn't feel dead. I don't think I had ever felt so alive. I kept swimming . . . and the island ahead grew bigger. I could see trees now, and a small hill. I swam closer. The seal had reached the island. It rocked up onto a flat rock that jutted out from the island, used its flippers like hands to raise itself up, then turned to watch me.

I wasn't scared of the seal now. I mean, not terrified. It was okay. It was helping me. Humans don't care about me, but animals do. Hannu was right. Animals watch over us. I slowed down swimming to the island and looked carefully. I couldn't see any signs of boats. There was no building behind the trees. No curl of smoke drifting into the sky. This was it, my own place. My own island. I kicked back my heels and swam the last bit, exhausted.

In those last few strokes I was panting like I'd run an ultra-marathon. I could make out trees, bushes, sandy beaches and sloping rocks. There was no sign of life. No boat. No summerhouse. I would rest here. I had to. I couldn't go on. If the Wild School staff came searching for me, I'd see them coming and I would hide. I was ace at hiding. I could crouch down and not move, not make a sound. I could slip into shadowy places. I could climb into trees. Trees made great hiding places – people never looked up.

In the next stroke my toes scraped over stones. I yelled out in relief. I'd made it! I wasn't going to drown. The people of Ahtola wouldn't cart my soul off to Tuonela:

the land of the dead. By now I was on my feet, panting in agony – I thought my chest would snap in two. I waded to the shore, ploughing back armfuls of ocean, reached the beach and fell headlong onto the sand, crying out in pain and exhaustion. I dragged myself up the sand and slumped forward.

Behind me, I heard a loud splash. I was too weary to be scared but looked round to see the seal's head rise from the water. It was watching me . . . then it slipped under the sea and vanished. My arms buckled under me and I collapsed onto the sand again. Every bone in my body was like jelly. Everything in me wanted to sleep for days, but this beach was too exposed. Even totally exhausted I had the wits to hide. So I dragged myself further up the beach on my belly and wriggled under a bush. I didn't care that it scratched me. I hardly noticed. I slumped my head down and plunged into a black sleep.

I slept in fits, maybe for hours, maybe minutes, I don't know. Feverish dreams haunted me. I could hear the drone of a giant wasp. Swarms of them coming closer. And men shouting. I could feel the ground under me move, like the sea. When I woke my throat was on fire with thirst and my mind jumpy with fear of being discovered. I had to find a better hiding place. And I had to find water. If it wasn't such agony it would be funny – boy stages incredible escape from Wild School only to die of thirst!

I forced myself to get out from under the bush. Wobbling, scratched and groggy, I got to my feet and headed away from the sea. It was a major effort to put one foot in front of the other, but I kept going, towards some trees, staggering like I was drunk. A gull screeched. I ducked. Then another bird swooped down. I shielded my head with my hands and yelled at them. That woke me up proper.

I hurried now, tramping over the heather, dodging dive-bombing sea birds and scanning the island for water. My senses were alert like a wolf. I had to drink. My mind spun. What time was it? The sun was rising. It could be three in the morning. I must have slept for hours under that bush. And what was the date? Suddenly it seemed important but I could hardly remember. The fifteenth of July, or the sixteenth? Something like that. My throat was parched. I sniffed the air, sure I could smell fresh water.

Suddenly there it was by the trees, like a silver thread in the moss: a small stream. Maybe this was a mirage. It shimmered like it wasn't real. Maybe thirst does this to you. Maybe swimming for kilometres does this. You want something so bad you imagine it.

I crept towards the stream, thinking with every trembling step how it would vanish before my crazy eyes. But it didn't. I got closer. Bracken and gorse bushes grazed my legs. I passed a clump of birch trees. The stream was still there, gurgling, sparkling, welling up from the ground and spilling fresh water into a small pool.

I fell headlong into the pool and drank. I drank loudly,

like a dog, lapping up the water. It tasted fantastic. I drank and drank. I scooped up water and flung it into the air. I whooped. I yelled.

Then I heard something behind me.

Chapter Sixteen

I froze. I felt like a wild animal. The front half of me was sprawled in the pool. Someone was behind me, I was convinced. Like a soldier in a jungle I dragged myself backward, not making a sound – I didn't want to be discovered with my face in a pool. Water dripped from my chin and I was scratched all over from the bushes that I had been lying in. I wanted to jump up, turn and run, but my body refused to move. Maybe whoever was behind me hadn't seen me. I pushed down so I was right in the heather and bushes, camouflaged. I lay like that for ages, not breathing hardly, not moving, my heart thumping.

Then I heard this awful howl. It burst out of the silence and cut right through me. That was no human. The howl sounded so sad – I have never heard anything like it. I turned round and there it was, the black seal, dragging itself over the heather. It was coming straight for me.

Now I saw how huge it was. Maybe it wasn't a seal.

Maybe I'd landed up on an island of monsters. Its haunting howl terrified me and I let out a strangled kind of cry – I couldn't help it. The creature kept coming, dragging its huge body, rocking over the heather, wailing like a ghost. If this was a seal it was massive.

I scrambled to my feet. Whimpering, I bolted away like I'd been hit by lightning, turning and running over the heather, away from the creature. My legs felt like jelly – I had swum for hours – and I was exhausted, petrified. I was starving. So I don't know where I found the energy. But I did. I fled. I had bare feet. They were cut. Thorns tore at my legs. I crashed through the bracken, not daring to look back in case the creature was right behind. I lunged for a tree and in a flash I scaled it, my heart a drum in my ribs. I was pretty sure the seal, or walrus or whatever it was, wouldn't be able to climb a tree. Just to make sure, I climbed right to the top. I was like an acrobat. Or a monkey. The branches creaked. I clung on and peered down.

Through the green leaves I could make out the creature. It was now basking in the early morning sun, lounging on a rock near the sea. It seemed to have forgotten me, thank God! I drew a branch back for a better look. It was black all over, and sleek. It had a smooth round head and a fat long body. And it was thudding its tail thing up and down on the rock, making a dull slapping sound. The huge creature looked like the seals in my books, and things I had read in those books came to me in a flash, like – seals are curious creatures. Seals will move towards humans, unlike many other wild animals.

Then I remembered Hannu's stories, about the man with the seal skin, and about the human and the seal being buried together. I felt like I'd landed in a magical world and a cold shiver crept over my skin.

I stayed in the tree. The seal stayed on the rock. It had stopped thudding its tail and nodding its head. Maybe it was asleep? I was dizzy with hunger. Maybe none of this was happening? Maybe I was imagining everything? I slapped my face, and it didn't hurt much. I scratched the back of my hand, wobbled a bit then grasped the branch.

I felt light-headed, scared I might fall out of the tree, then I would die and all this great effort would have been for nothing. I had to get out of the tree. It looked as if the creature was asleep . . . I had to eat something. Berries, even. I had seen some blueberries in the bushes, and I was suddenly gripped by this overwhelming need to devour loads of berries.

I slipped down the trunk of the tree. I was stealth itself! I jumped and landed without a sound on the carpet of pine needles. The blueberry bushes were clumped about near the seal. Great! I stood still as a statue and watched it. Its eyes were closed. It was slumped down over the bushes. Like a thief I approached the massive black creature until I was so close I could see its long silver whiskers. And folds in its leathery dark skin. And grey blotches under the black. I saw the rise and fall of its huge breathing body. I could smell it, strong and animal.

I edged around it, the plump dark blueberries calling to me like wallets in the market square used to call me. Nicking wallets felt like years ago, like another lifetime. I glanced down at the mighty creature and suddenly it opened one yellow eye, bared its teeth and then I really did scream.

The scream came out all husky and strangled. I bolted around the thing and ran for the sea. I forgot about food as I pelted over the bushes, the heather, the sand and over the flat rocks. Then I jumped into the sea. I swam a few strokes then stopped.

'*Don't worry, Niilo.*' It was Hannu's voice I heard calling to me. '*It's watching over you.*' That's what he was saying. '*One day you'll find your wild song,*' he said, '*then you'll know where freedom is.*' Where was he? He wasn't here. There was no boat. His voice was in my head. '*It won't hurt you,*' he said, and I knew he meant the seal. The fear drained out of me.

I twisted round, but the creature wasn't stirring. I swam back to the shore and pushed myself up onto a rock. The creature was still watching me, but it hadn't bothered to move. I clung onto Hannu's voice – '*Don't worry, Niilo. Everything is going to work out fine*' – and I didn't feel terrified with his voice in my head. The seal rolled over on the heather. It was making itself comfortable, like it was making itself a bed. It lowered its black head down and closed its eyes. Right now, all it seemed interested in was sleep.

And suddenly that seemed like the best idea in the world. I know it was light, but it was still the middle of the night. Tiredness washed over me like a wave. I yawned and slumped down in the bracken. I yawned again. I couldn't keep my eyes open one second longer . . .

'. . . *it was once a huge kingdom, Niilo, the sea kingdom of Ahtola, but there are very few people of the sea left. Like wolves. Like bears. Like honey bees. Like dinosaurs. They disappear. But some are still with us. When we stand on the edge of our fear they come to us. When we need help, they help us. When it seems that we might die they come to save us. I believe that. Do you, Niilo? They know the wild song. They watch over us.*'

They watch over us. My heart pounded hard. I rubbed my eyes and sat up. I heard a splashing noise. I was so tired, and confused that I couldn't work out where I was. The dream fled. And where was Hannu? I called out his name and heard my voice echo back: '*Hannu! Hannu!*' I heard the splash again and I blinked and saw the creature in the sea. All I could see was its black head, sticking up out of the water.

'*A husband and wife perhaps, or twins . . . but it wasn't, it was a man and a seal.*'

It was a man and a seal. A shiver ran over my skin. Hannu's voice spoke in my head, as loud and clear as if he was sitting right next to me: '*There's more to life than*

114

what we see. Much more, Niilo. Know why I think you've come to the Wild School? Because something's missing. You're looking for magic. You've lost your song. You want more out of life. Me too, Niilo. Me too.'

I gulped in air, my heart kicking, my palms sweating. Maybe Hannu was right? Maybe the old stories were true? Something *was* missing. Everything was missing. I couldn't peel my eyes away from the creature in the sea. Now the thing lifted its sleek black head and turned its head from side to side. Maybe none of this was real? Maybe I was dreaming the whole thing? I looked at my hands and I imagined Hannu's clenched fist pounding into the soil. Maybe I was going mad?

I called for him again. 'Hannu! Hannu!' I could feel hot tears streaming down my face but I didn't care. I'd never felt so lonely. I was the only person on this island and I felt like the last person in the world. I felt miserable.

'Know why you've come to the Wild School?' Well, I wasn't on the Wild School. God knows where I was. Some rock with a clump of trees and a wild animal with yellow eyes and fangs instead of teeth that is way too interested in me. It's planning me for its next meal. No one had bothered to search for me. They didn't care. They didn't send out the helicopters. Too expensive for the bad boy. They didn't send out the lifeboats. They were probably having a party in the Wild School right now.

I lay down, pounded the ground with my fists, and howled.

Chapter Seventeen

I must have cried myself to sleep. I dreamt the drowning dream again. I was reaching out through the water, trying to grab at someone's hand. My throat clammed up with terror. Then the hand vanished. In my sleep I tried to reach for that hand. But the hand wasn't there.

When I woke, sweating, the sun was already high in the sky. I was hot. Then I was shivering with cold. My heart was hammering. I told myself it was only a dream. I didn't drown. I'd swum in the sea and I hadn't drowned. I grabbed at clumps of moss and draped it over me. The exhaustion came back. I resisted sleep in case the drowning dream returned, but I couldn't resist for long. Sleep sucked me like water down a drainpipe.

Hours later I woke, blinking in the bright light. The horrible fear I had felt earlier had gone. Now I felt relaxed. I had survived one night and what felt like most of the next day, and I was still alive. I heard gulls screech above me and I felt my chest pressed against springy heather and soft moss. I lay there, face down, not moving, still drowsy with sleep, feeling weird, all light like a balloon. Eventually I opened one eye and stared at a bright green blade of grass. It was a millimetre from my eye. For ages I lay there staring at that one blade of grass. It was huge. It was like a sword. There was a tiny insect crawling up it and I studied it, like it was the most fascinating thing in the world. The tiny insect took ages, and sometimes it slid down a bit, then started over. Then I became vaguely aware that there was more in the world than a tiny insect and a towering blade of grass. There was more grass. I opened my other eye and lifted my head, then I dragged myself along on my front, like I'd seen the creature do. I felt like a paratrooper slinking along in enemy country in the long grass. Finally I rolled over, sat up and did a quick scan of my surroundings.

I was on my island. There was a lot of grass, and bushes, and further off a clump of pine and birch trees, like on the Wild School, but different. The Wild School island had the human touch, with its rope bridges, benches, piers, buildings and stuff. This island that I had swum to didn't. That was what I had wanted but it was pretty scary. Not a house. Not a road. Not a wooden bench. No electricity. Not a person. Not a boat. Not a rope bridge. I swallowed hard. This was a real Wild Island – Niilo's island.

I rose to my knees and looked for the seal. I couldn't see it anywhere. It wasn't lounging about on the rock. It wasn't slinking around in the sea. That made me uneasy, not knowing where it was, but I didn't feel frightened. Maybe it was the long sleep that had calmed me. And the fact I had drunk half the fresh water in the pool. I think a whole night had passed – maybe half the next day too? The sun was high in the sky. Maybe the seal had left the island? Maybe, and I liked this thought, it had been one of those magical creatures from Ahtola – those creatures Hannu spoke about – and it had guided me to this island and just hung around to check I was okay. It had been watching over me.

Maybe I really was going mad, but that version sounded like a possibility. Just when I was feeling relaxed about being watched over, another thought popped into my head. It wouldn't want to eat me, would it? I batted that mad thought away. I had read the books and I knew seals didn't eat humans, but part of me feared that anything could happen on this island. And nobody would know. Or care.

I looked down at my body – suntanned, torn shorts, scratches everywhere and looking pretty skinny. If I didn't eat soon I'd be skin and bones. I'd only been gone one or two days and already I *looked* wild. There were still amazingly a few streaks of grease on my arms. And I felt ravenous. I had planned on gorging myself on berries. Now I couldn't remember whether I had eaten any the night before or not.

'Breakfast time,' I said – out loud, just for the company. My voice sounded tiny. I staggered up to my feet, realising that I still felt wobbly. I took a few steps, and a few deep breaths. I was beginning to feel like a real castaway. Good thing I had learnt to pick berries and dandelion leaves, fir-tree sprouts and nettles at the Wild School, and to know which were poisonous and which were good. I set out over the springy bushes in search of food . . . and I didn't have far to go. I grabbed at a few dandelion leaves and crunched them down. They tasted sweet. I crammed fistfuls into my mouth. Then it was time for pudding. I looked down at the bushes and spied the small round dark berries. Blueberries. I could see the bushes flattened out, where the seal had been sleeping. I saw again, by its imprint, how huge it was. I forgot about monster seals and grabbed a berry. The juice burst in my mouth with a zing, so I ate more, scrambling over the ground, grabbing at berries and shoving them into my mouth. It took a lot to make me feel full. And when I was I fell down, rolled over and gazed up at the blue sky. A few flies droned above me. Drowsily I swatted them away.

I still felt uneasy at the edges about loads of things – like the huge seal, the nightmare, Hannu getting married, and a search party coming to look for me, and my parents getting told I had drowned, and maybe my name being in the newspapers. I liked to imagine the whole of Finland searching for me, and here I was chilled out and just doing my thing. I wondered what picture of me would be in the papers. I wondered if I was on TV. I wondered what my mum would say, if the journalists came and interviewed her. '*I loved him so much,*' she would say, crying buckets.

'*I gave him everything.*' None of that seemed real. The only thing that was real was the sharp taste of blueberries in my mouth and the scratchy heather under my back. It felt so good to lie back and stare up at the sky. To have my belly full of food, and not plastic food from some supermarket, but food I had hunted for with my own hands. And it felt great to have my very own island.

Maybe this was it? This was the life I had always been waiting for, preparing for? I took slow deep breaths and lay there feeling perfect bliss for about ten minutes. Then I began to wonder, and doubt, and worry.

I was all alone.

When I let that thought sink in it scared me. For years I'd vanished into my capsule. I was used to feeling alone. But as I gazed about, over the pine trees and heather and out to the blue ring of sea, it hit me that for the first time ever, I was *really* alone. Scary. But exciting too. I had just got used to the idea that I was alone when I had another thought. Maybe I wasn't? Maybe this wasn't my very own island? I mean, I hadn't checked the whole island out yet. I got up and picked bits of heather out of my hair. I would need to explore. Maybe there was a summer-house tucked away, or a small hut? Maybe there was a helicopter landing pad? Maybe this island belonged to a film star? An artist? A hermit? Or an axe murderer? I took a few hesitant steps and stubbed my toes against a stone. It hurt. And I was shivering with cold – the sun was warm, but there was a cool wind off the sea. Apart from these baggy black swimming shorts, I was naked. I had been so tired, and thirsty, and hungry, I hadn't noticed that I was cold. I looked around helplessly, like a hoodie might miraculously appear out of thin air, and a pair of trainers, my size.

That's when it really hit me: that I had managed to swim to another island. I had escaped and now I was alone. No money. Apart from leaves and berries, no food. Apart from shorts, no clothes. Apart from moss and springy bushes, no bed. Apart from one mysterious animal that now seemed to have vanished, no company.

I kept glancing over my shoulder as I walked over the springy heather. My feet hurt from the scratches, but I quickly learnt to place my bare feet in soft moss, or on flat stones. And the more I explored the less nervous I felt. It was like I was growing taller and stronger. This was my island. There was nobody here and nothing to worry about. I'd been told how there were thousands of islands in the Finnish Archipelago and most of them were uninhabited. I punched the air. By this time I was pretty sure my little island was one of the undiscovered. I felt great. I didn't care about anything. This was it: the thing worth fighting for – freedom! I whooped loudly.

I heard my voice carry over the island and waited for somebody to appear. No one did. I strode off over the heather and walked to the top of a small hill. From here I could see the whole island. There was no hut. No house. No wisp of smoke. I lifted my arms into the air, flexed my small hard muscles. I was king of this world. And I felt better than I ever felt. I had beaten my fear of the sea. I had swum to freedom. I had survived. I shouted like a crazy boy – 'I'm free!!!'

My voice didn't sound tiny now. It sounded huge. Maybe the wild animal thought I was in trouble? Maybe it thought I was calling it back? Whatever it thought, the wild animal that was either a seal or a walrus or a mythical beast came back.

Chapter Eighteen

I stood on the top of the hill and watched it. I saw its round black head way off in the sea. It swam towards the island. In a weird way the creature seemed familiar. And in another weird way, I was almost happy to see it again. Was I so starved for company that even a seal was better than being totally alone? Or maybe because I felt so good and strong and free, I thought I could handle anything. Anyway, it slid onto the pebbly beach – a fat long sleek thing. It had two stunted arms. Flat hands. It dragged its heavy body up the beach with these spread-out hands. I had a good view of it and I felt like a visitor had entered my private island. Maybe it comes every day to snuggle down in the heather? Maybe it likes sunbathing on that flat rock? Maybe this isn't my private island? It is the creature's private island. My mind raced. I sunk down onto my knees, wondering what my visitor would do next.

It lifted its head and the black animal looked straight at me. Pushing down on its hands (from where I stood they looked like hands!), it pushed the upper half of its body up high, lifted back its head and stared at me. That freaked me out, getting eyeballed like that, and I could feel my knees tremble. But I held its gaze. I didn't faint or keel over and suddenly I got the strangest sensation. Images, like fast-moving film, flashed into my head. A boat. A man. A child. And then towering waves. I didn't understand it. It was like the seal was planting these pictures in my head. These were pictures from my nightmare. I felt a shiver creep over my skin. But I kept staring.

I was a master starer. I could win battles just by shooting the evil eye at people. But this was different. This was an animal. The weird pictures in my head vanished. As I stood there on the top of the hill the creature dragged itself up the stony beach and onto the springy heather. There was something totally prehistoric about the way it moved. Beneath my ribs, my heart pounded, and the hairs on my arms prickled. But I didn't flinch. Sometimes the creature dropped its head to concentrate on where it was going. Sometimes it looked up, as if it was checking that I was still there.

'Just think, Niilo, a man and a seal, buried together, one hand on top of the other, five thousand years ago. We were brothers, back then.'

It had managed to haul itself over the heather. It stopped at the flattened patch where it had slept the day before. It lifted its head and sniffed. Then it rocked itself around and headed back down to the sea. I watched it slide into the water again and felt a tiny slither of disappointment, like I had believed my story. I had imagined this really was some magical guardian come to look over me. But it had lost interest.

I was curious now. The seal called me like a magnet calls a pin. I ran down the hillside, over the beach, then slowed when I came to the rocks. The black thing was swimming round and round like it was waiting for me. It lifted its head and looked in my direction. Sometimes it made funny blowing sounds. It didn't look like a monster at all. More like a dog. I suddenly got the feeling it wanted to play with me.

I was feeling brave and strong, so I hooted, like I remembered it had done yesterday, or was it the day before? It seemed to study me, then it howled back. It kicked up its tail fins and dived under the water. I ran a few more steps over the flat rocks. Then suddenly it broke the surface of the water and – I couldn't believe it – it had a fish between its teeth. Beads of red blood around its mouth gleamed in the sun. The seal swam towards me and flung the fish at my feet, then flipped round and swam off.

I stared down at the fish. Its silvery body trembled. It jerked its tail back and forth, then suddenly stopped. A wide round eye stared up at me. This was a present. I was supposed to eat this dead thing. Its silvery scales had tints of blue and red – it was like a small rainbow. I knew if I was serious about surviving on this island I would have to eat fish. I glanced up at the seal. It had its black head lifted out of the water, like it was waiting to see what I was going to do. I looked back at the gift of fish, and swallowed hard.

Hannu had tried to teach me how to build fires. He had held a piece of glass next to tinder dry grasses and miraculously the grasses had caught fire. He had said it was the sun's reflection. I remembered he'd brought little twigs and made a spire shape. He had been busy while I had stood doing nothing. I'd watched him gut a fish. Then he'd speared the fish onto a stick. It had been that simple. He'd said this was the way our ancestors survived. And how he and I had the north in our blood. We knew the ways of nature, deep down inside, he'd said. It was just a question of remembering. He'd held the fish over the flames then, till I could smell the flesh singe. It had caught in the back of my throat and made me feel sick. I had watched him flick its charred body back and forth. To make sure it was all cooked through, he'd said. I'd thought it was disgusting, and I had told Hannu there was no way I would ever eat that. 'Suit yourself, Niilo.' That's what he had said, biting into it. 'You don't know what you're missing,' he'd said.

'Gross.' That's what I'd said then.

I gaped at the fish now. I was as wide-eyed as it. Hunger gnawed inside me. I was starving. Time was a blur, but I reckoned I had been away from the Wild School for two and a half days. In all that time I had eaten a few dandelion leaves and a pile of blueberries, and that was all. The seal was swimming back and forth. It was watching me, probably to see what I was going to do with the present. 'Okay,' I shouted out to it. 'I'll eat it.' I bent down and touched the fish, then I pulled my hand back and shuddered – it felt flabby, cold and revolting.

I looked up at the seal. It was looking back at me. Suddenly it hit me that this wasn't a game. This was my life now and I had better get used to it. No van was going to pull up blaring out rock music and selling kebabs. I took a deep breath and forced myself to pick up the fish. I winced at the slippery feel of it, but told myself not to be a wimp. I had a pocket in my shorts and I stuffed the fish into my pocket – I didn't want any hungry gulls swooping down and making off with it. Hurriedly I gathered twigs, then pulled up the driest grasses I could find. I searched the stony beach near the rocks for glass. Hannu said you could often find just what you needed brought in by the tide, if you really looked for it. Maybe this was beginner's luck, or maybe that seal creature really was my guardian from Ahtola, but I found a small piece of broken glass.

I set up the twigs into a little spire. I bunched the dry grasses together, angled the glass between the sun and the grass, and moved it about. This was the hardest bit. Ages passed and the fish was probably going off in my pocket. Who did I think I was? Robinson Crusoe? Just when I thought this would never ever work, it did. Suddenly I smelt burning and saw a tiny wisp of smoke in the bunch of grass. I couldn't believe it! It had caught. The smoke snarled into a tiny flame and I had done it! Like my ancient ancestors from deepest darkest Finland, I had made fire!

Then I had to gut the thing. That was the grossest part. Hannu had used a knife. I used a twig, stripping the bark from it. It was pretty sharp, so I stabbed the end of the twig into the belly of the fish. It went in smoothly, like a knife slicing into a cake. I tugged the twig upwards, then the fish opened up and all these innards spewed out. I just got on with the job, all the time remembering how Hannu had done it and trying not to feel sick. I scooped out the guts. Then I stabbed the fish right through with the twig and dangled it over the flames, batting a few droning flies off. 'Buzz off!' I yelled. 'This is my fish!'

Just like the berries, pulled from the bushes with my own hands, this fish – gutted and cooked over a fire I had made – tasted fantastic. I forgot I didn't even like fish. The warm tasty flesh seemed to melt in my mouth, and I ate every scrap from the thin bones. I was so hungry I even sucked on the head. All black and charred from the fire it didn't look like a head. Then I threw the skeleton away. It didn't even reach the ground – it was immediately snatched up by a gull. They'd already made off with the guts.

When there was nothing left to eat I ran back to the rocks and searched for the seal. I was still hungry – I could have eaten *ten* fish. The seal, my fish provider, was now asleep on its rock. Was that all it ever did? Sleep? It had taken me ages to cook that fish. I probably used up more energy making the fire and gutting the fish than I got from eating it and I was still starving. I had to have more. I shouted at the seal, 'I'm still hungry.' It was like the summer breeze snatched at my voice and drowned it. I thought about pelting the creature with a stone to wake it up. 'I'm starving,' I yelled, snatching up a pebble. I drew back my arm, aiming to hit the seal, but something made my fingers fall open. The stone dropped. Something weird was going on. I backed away, goose bumps running up my arms.

I turned and ran over the heather. Sure, I was still ravenous, but even one fish had given me some energy. I felt strong. I didn't know where I was headed, but I took off over the island. Maybe I would find mushrooms? Would there be mushrooms in mid-July? Or raspberries? In minutes I had reached the other side. My island was seriously not big.

Ahead of me was a small dark clump of trees. I made for the trees, and that's when I found the wooden hut. I almost yelled out, and smacked my hand over my mouth. The old hut was hidden away, ringed by tall dark pine trees. I forgot all about fish and starvation and pressed back against a tree. The hut looked so wrecked I doubted anybody was home, but if they were I didn't want them bumping into an escaped convict from the Wild School prison. Half the roof was broken, the door hung open, and the windows were broken. This might have been some-body's summerhouse a hundred years ago. Now it looked like a summerhouse for ghosts and bandits, and I don't know which I was most scared of.

I held onto Hannu's voice in my head, like a lifeline – '*Don't worry, Niilo. The magical creatures of Ahtola are watching over you.*' I bit my lip and looked about. There were no signs of life. No flattened-down grass. No litter. The grass had grown up at the door. Nobody had been through that door for a long time. I took a few wary steps towards it. 'Is anybody there?'

Adrenalin pumped through my body. By this time I was pretty convinced there was nobody there. No ghosts. No bandits. This could be *my* hut, though I would have to patch it up a bit. I tingled all over. This was better than filching purses, way better than stealing wallets. Better than the scariest movie.

'Anybody there?' I said again.

The door creaked in the breeze. I jumped, then laughed. Nobody there but the wind. I sidled up to the front of the hut. By this time I could stretch out my arm and touch the dilapidated old place. I did. The wood felt warm. I stepped forward and forced myself to peer through the broken window. What a dump! The inside of the hut had just one room and it looked like seagull heaven. I tapped on what was left of the window and two huge gulls panicked and took off, through the hole in the roof. What a racket their flapping wings made! I stuck my head through the gap in the broken window. What a stink! The place was full of bird droppings. I held my nose and peered in.

It was pretty gloomy inside because of the trees around it. But I could see in the middle of the hut there was a broken bed and the stuffing was pulled out of the mattress. I could see stains all over the blue and white striped mattress. On the floor there were little mounds of earth, some broken dishes, a couple of dead birds and a pile of magazines.

I pushed back the door, pinched my nose and stepped in, disturbing another bird inside. It flapped about dementedly before taking off through the hole in the roof. Then I was alone. The place was silent. Stinking. Gloomy. Creepy. I just stood there in the shadowy stink, letting the place settle around me. Then I let go of holding my nose. The smell wasn't too terrible once you got used to it. I picked up one of the magazines. It was a women's magazine. Ancient. The yellow paper smelt mouldy. I flicked through it. Cake recipes. Knitting patterns. Romantic stories. I stepped over the mounds of earth, bird poo, broken plates and dead birds.

A rotting cupboard door hung on its hinges. The reek of damp coming from behind it was sickening but I forced myself to look inside. And there it was: a brown faded shirt. Considering it was prehistoric it wasn't a complete rag. I took it off the nail it hung on and put it on. It was way too big for me, but it would do. Then I rummaged about for a pair of shoes. I couldn't find any, but I did find a lighter, stubs of candle, three tins of tomato soup, a battered white enamel cup and a packet of mouldy biscuits stored away in a tin. The biscuits had turned green. I gulped and swung round, convinced someone was about to step inside. The door creaked again in the wind.

'Calm down, Niilo,' I said out loud. 'Some old fisherman was here. But he's not now. He's gone. Look at this dump. I mean, who would want to come here?' Talking to myself helped. I calmed down and had another rummage around in the cupboard. I found more evidence of recent life: a packet of coffee that still smelt like coffee. An empty packet of cigarettes. An open penknife that wasn't totally rusted. I shut the penknife up, swiped it and put it in my pocket – it had been a hard job gutting the fish with twigs. I swiped the lighter as well. I looked at the packet of cigarettes, grabbed it and shook it as a sudden urge to smoke came over me, even though I hadn't smoked for three months. I flung the empty packet of cigarettes away. For a moment I felt mad, then a bird flapped about above the roof and I forgot about smoking. I yelled at it and it flew off.

Under the broken window there was a wooden shelf. On it stood a blackened pot and about twenty stubs of white candles. Next to the pot was a book. I picked it up and read the front cover. *Moominland Midwinter*, it said, by Tove Jansson. I opened it and fingered the thin paper. I remembered the Moomins, and I got this sudden warm feeling about Moomin Mama and Papa and the whole happy family. I considered stuffing the book into the pocket of my shorts. Maybe I would take one of the magazines too?

But I forgot about nicking reading material when my eyes fell on a pretty smart-looking green fishing rod. It was propped up against the wall, beside the bed. What else did a castaway need? I had it all: fire, knife, fishing rod, shirt. I grabbed the rod.

The door creaked again, louder this time, and a shiver shot up my spine. I dropped the book, jumped over the pile of magazines, kicked a mound of earth and dashed out. What a relief to be outside! The stink had gone. The dark creepy mood had gone. I hurried away, wearing my new brown shirt and grasping a fishing rod. If the seal was only going to fling me one fish a day I was going to have to fend for myself.

I made for the shore. I was still hungry. And I had the taste for barbecued fish now. It didn't matter that I wasn't clued up on fishing – I thought you just stuck a worm on the hook, dipped it in the water and miraculously it would catch fish.

I fell to the ground and dug with my bare hands in the earth, searching for worms. I found two that way. Then I copied what the gulls did. I drummed my fingers on the ground, like I was rain, and amazingly three fat worms fell for that trick and appeared. I shoved four of the pink wriggling worms in my pocket and hooked one for bait. I felt pretty squeamish doing that, but when you've got this deep gnawing hunger growling away inside you, there's one thing you do know. You *have* to eat.

Somehow, if you are going to survive, you have to eat.

Chapter Nineteen

The sun was high in the sky. I had lost track of time. Maybe it was late afternoon on the second day. I planned to try my hand at fishing off the rocks, but before setting off for the shore I headed up the hill. This was going to be my lookout point and I would need to scan the horizon every hour or so. It felt good to have a plan.

Once I got up there I did a three hundred and sixty degree turn, hand above my eyes like I was some sea captain. Way in the distance I saw tiny white dots, like doll's handkerchiefs. They were yachts. From where I was they looked like toys. Probably holidaymakers. People having fun with nothing to worry about. Happy people sailing around with plenty of food stored away, and drink, and cigarettes. I turned my back on them. They weren't coming to get me.

I scanned the skies for helicopters, rescue planes. All I could see was a wheeling white gull. Was I so unimportant that they hadn't even called out a search party? I kicked at a clump of tufted grass as hot tears pricked at my eyes. With bare feet, even kicking grass hurt. Feeling totally sorry for myself I headed down the hill.

A good while later I felt even sorrier – and I wanted to fling the stupid useless fishing rod into the sea. A hundred times I had dipped it into the water and brought it up empty a hundred times. I'd used up all the disgusting worms and I couldn't stomach getting more. My arm was aching. There were fish in the bay, I knew there were. The lazy fat seal slept on. I don't know how many times I burst into tears. I hadn't cried for years. Since landing on this island two days ago I had been in tears at least ten times. I shouted. I swore. I punched myself. I wanted to karate-chop the ancient fishing rod, but instead I clutched onto it like it was my lifeline.

I did have a lifeline, but it wasn't the fishing rod. It was that black sleeping seal over on the rock. I must have cried myself to sleep. A castaway learns fast – sleeping conserves energy, so when you can't eat you might as well sleep. Maybe that was why the seal spent most of the day asleep. The sun was sinking down the sky when I woke. Before I even opened my eyes I sniffed. Like an animal I sniffed again. There was something wafting in my nostrils that reminded me of the stalls in the market. I turned my head, opened my eyes, and there it was: a plump little gift. In fact, two little gifts. Two fish, lined up next to me.

The seal was gone.

Chapter Twenty

Using the lighter was much easier than trying to get a spark from the sun, especially as the sun was setting. I cooked myself a great supper. What a feast! And the brown shirt I now had on kept the chill away. I half considered sleeping in the creepy hut, but I was too full of food and too tired to move. And it didn't look like it was going to rain. The mammoth swim must have really zapped my energy as I seemed to be doing nothing but sleeping, and if I wasn't sleeping I was eating, or thinking about eating. Life was suddenly very simple.

I lay down in the heather and gazed up at the reddening sky. I thought vaguely how I should have some kind of plan. I mean, I couldn't stay on this island for ever, could I? What about somehow stowing away on a ferry bound for Sweden? I remembered the street performer and his hat of coins. The world, I thought, was my oyster. Wasn't that what people said when they meant you could do whatever you liked, go wherever you liked. Then I yawned. Even thinking was too much like hard work. I yawned again, closed my eyes, rolled over on the heather and slept.

The drowning dream came again. Maybe it was the constant hum of the sea. Maybe it was the after-effects of having swum for a whole day in the sea. But it was the same hand, the same bleak terror, the same feeling of my throat clamped up, water swirling and the hand vanishing. The same child I had seen when I stared at the seal. The same boat. The same man. Maybe I called out in my sleep? Maybe I thrashed my arms up and down in the heather, because when I woke at dawn I wasn't alone.

The black seal was close by, and watching me. Its huge yellow eyes stared at me and I stared back. It was about ten metres away and I could smell it, though it didn't smell bad, more like seaweed. I could see each long whisker and how the animal had black nostrils and folds of skin over its eyes and a kind, almost human expression. I felt like I should be terrified, but I just lay there, gazing at it.

I wasn't scared, even though I had never been this close to a wild animal – even in the zoo you couldn't get that near. I told myself I should be worried, but I just lay there, on my side, looking at the seal. I stared into its huge yellow eyes and it was like I could see all kinds of things reflected in those eyes: mountains, huge ice-cold lakes, snow, bears, fires. It was like I could see myself, and Hannu, and the sea, and the moon and stars and the aurora borealis. I even saw my mum. I saw a man with her, and a young boy. He looked like me. Then I saw the man and boy sink under the sea, like in my nightmare. I should have been scared, but I wasn't. Just really sad.

The seal rocked over the heather towards me and, although I could feel my heart thud as it came closer, I didn't move. Even if I wanted to move I don't know if I could have. All the time it kept gazing at me and I remembered the words Hannu said – how everything was going to be all right. It was like the seal was saying it too. And I remember Hannu saying I needed to find my story. I had the sudden mad thought that this seal was my storyteller. It was giving me my lost story. I can't remember anything ever before looking at me like that. So loving. That's the only word for it. And the seal was so close I could reach out and touch it . . .

They were buried holding hands – that's what Hannu said. And how it was a true story. Slowly I stretched my arm forward. The seal didn't flinch. Moving with great stillness I pushed myself towards the animal. The way it looked at me felt like the seal was saying – *yes, come*. So I reached out and gently touched its flipper. I thought its flipper would feel slimy but it didn't. It felt warm, so alive, just like thick strong skin. I lay my hand over its hand, and it let me.

That's when I started to believe in animal magic. That's when I stopped doing the hate-stare. That's when I knew something wonderful and mysterious was looking after me. It felt like a mother soothing a child from a nightmare. Its eyes seemed to see right inside me – it seemed to have such a human face – and I saw it had five fingers. We were the same, this animal of the sea and me. I suddenly had this weird sensation that me and the seal were brothers. I felt peaceful. I felt like I wasn't thirteen years old any longer, but hundreds of years old. I didn't know what was happening to me but I didn't fight it. The seal nodded its head. I nodded my head, and my eyelids drooped.

I must have fallen asleep again. When I woke it was daylight and the seal was gone. Maybe that had been a dream too – the black seal lying close to me, letting me touch its hand – but it had felt real. It felt more real than anything else. And inside me I had what felt like a page of my story. Call it magic. Call me weird. But the seal knew something I didn't know, and it was trying to tell me. From way out at sea I heard a deep and haunting call. I sat up and waved. It was the seal. I was convinced now, more than ever, that this creature was watching over me.

It was now my third or fourth day as a castaway. There were a few clouds in the sky, but the weather was still warm. For something to do I walked round the island a few times and started noticing little things I hadn't noticed before: tiny little pink and yellow flowers and sloping flat rocks. It was on one of my walks round my island that I discovered a tiny beach. It was hidden round the back of the island and the sand there was white. You could believe no human had set foot on this pure beach. In front of the beach was a small bay fringed with smooth rocks. There wasn't a ripple on the water.

I was gazing out to sea, doing my usual scanning the horizon thing and thinking how I would call this place Horseshoe Bay, when suddenly I heard this *plop* sound. That gave me a jolt. Next thing, I saw a big fish jump out of the water and slap back in again – *plop*! Then another. Horseshoe Bay was teeming with fish, and not just little fish: they were huge. Okay, so the fishing rod was useless – didn't mean I was. I was pretty skilled in picking things, wasn't I?

So I waded silently into the water. Seaweed swirled around my legs but it didn't bother me. By the time I was waist-deep I could see them – big fat silver fish. I guessed they weren't used to people as one even brushed my leg. I stood as still as a statue, my hands ready just above the surface. I waited for a fish, and didn't have to wait long. I saw one swim right towards me and I waited till the fish was right next to me, then shot my hands down through the water, cupped round the fish, squeezed and brought it up. What a beauty! I held on tight and waded fast out of the water, the thing twitching in my hands. By the time I reached the beach the fish had gone limp. Behind me I heard another deep *plop* sound. I swung round to see the seal. 'I did it,' I yelled, lifting up my catch. 'I caught it with my hands!'

I cooked it too. 'Thanks, fish,' I said to the last tasty piece of barbecued fish. 'You were delicious – thanks!'

By the time the sun was sinking in the sky that day I was hungry again. I went back to the bay, but all the fish had gone. So I wandered around a bit, picked a few tiny raspberries then went off to visit the hut.

I read three romantic stories from the old magazines and a chapter of *Moominland Midwinter*. On the jacket of the book it said that Tove Jansson had lived on a tiny island. I got this shiver up my spine, as if maybe this had been her island? She was a famous writer, the book said, and she was dead now. I liked the idea that she had lived on this island, writing books. Maybe she wrote the Moomins series in this hut? And maybe this had been her tomato soup? I kept thinking about the soup, wondering what it would taste like. I couldn't believe I was hungry again. It seemed like I was always hungry.

I checked again when she died and worked out it can't have been Tove Jansson's soup. Whoever's soup it was, I spent ages hacking away trying to open a tin of it. Finally I managed to pierce the tin with the knife. I tried to forget it was two years out of date as I poured the red, cold and pretty revolting soup down my throat. Soon as I'd eaten it I wished I hadn't. It tasted metallic, and definitely off. But it did dull the raging hunger, a bit. Then I climbed to the lookout point.

I told myself I was looking for boats, but really I was looking for the seal. When I couldn't find the seal I roamed the island, gorging myself on berries. I tried to ignore the gripping feeling in my stomach, tried not to think about the tomato soup – two years out of date.

I ran back to the lookout. I didn't see boats, or the seal,

but I did see heavy clouds coming in. It had been sunny for days. Okay, there had been a cool breeze sometimes, but this felt different. I looked down to the ring of trees and saw how the birch branches bent with the wind. It felt like a storm was coming. The weather didn't take long to break. The clouds rolled in, dark and fat, and let loose fat drops of rain. The clouds brought a gloomy darkness with them, and I was beginning to feel sick. I was cold and miserable. Why didn't the seal come and comfort me? Why did people, and creatures, get close to me, then disappear? Maybe I really was a monster? I remembered my dad's words – '*It's like living with a monster in the house.*' What was wrong with me?

'What's wrong?' I shouted. But there was no one to rage at. So I shouted again. To the rain. To the dark clouds. To the choppy sea.

I got soaked. And the rain didn't stop. It got heavier. Huge splatting drops the size of eyeballs. I tried to shelter under a tree. That didn't work. I tried to push myself in against the side of a rock. That didn't work either. I was drenched, totally miserable and shivering. My hair was plastered against my face and the smelly brown shirt was soaked and sticking to me. I couldn't stop shaking.

There was nothing else for it. That night I went to the hut.

Chapter Twenty-one

I pushed open the creaky door of the hut, my heart pounding. The rain was lashing at my back. In front of me the eerie hut was gloomy and smelly. But I had to find shelter so I stepped inside. It was pretty dark in there, which was just as well. Meant I couldn't see all the cobwebs, dead mice and bird poo. There was even something comforting about the little hut. Even though rain dripped through a corner of the roof, it was more or less dry. It was a shelter, and by this stage I wasn't fussy. It was too gross to sleep on the mattress, but there were two scabby moth-eaten blankets and a bit of dry floor, and I was used to sleeping on hard floors.

I found a wooden box with old newspapers inside. I dragged the box across the floor and hunched down in the one dry corner, between the wall and the box. The floorboards creaked under me as I rolled myself up in the blankets. I still felt wet through, but what could I do? I lay there, shivering and trying to sleep. Lightning suddenly flashed and for a split-second the hut dazzled bright white and electric blue. I saw the stained mattress, the hanging door at the cupboard, the skeleton of a bird, all lit up.

Then I was plunged back into the gloom. Shuddering, I wrapped myself tighter. It felt like summer was over. It had been light for so long, but now I lay trembling in the dark, and I was so cold I was shaking. I blew into my hands, wrapped my arms tight around me, but my teeth still wouldn't stop chattering. I had piled a few magazines up for a pillow so I closed my eyes and tried to sleep. If my bed wasn't so uncomfortable and the stink of the place so terrible, I might have found the whole scene funny. I thought about the rubbishy romantic stories under my cheek and the housewives fifty years ago desperate to make feather-light sponge cakes, to run off in the moonlight with tall dark strangers on horseback, and knit terrible chunky sweaters to keep warm in – I wished I had one now!

Rain fell through the roof but my corner stayed dry. The splatting rain almost felt like company, like I'd switched on some drumbeat music. *Splat-splat – splatsplatsplat*. I wondered where the seal was. *Splat-splat*. Eventually I stopped shaking and felt a wave of sleepiness wash over me. I pulled the blanket up over my face, to get away from the stink, and to be hidden in case the old fisherman suddenly turned up, searching for his tomato soup. I tried to forget I had rancid soup inside me – it was probably rotting my gut, probably slowly killing me, and after surviving this far it would be a shame to die of tomato soup . . . *Splatsplatsplat.* Sleep tugged me under. I didn't know if it was night or morning. The rain still drummed on the roof. My last thought was that I hoped I wouldn't have the drowning dream again.

I thought I was dreaming. I thought someone was running towards me, footsteps crunching over pebbles and twigs, crushing shells. But my eyes were open and I was staring into the blanket – it smelt damp. My neck was stiff. But I was awake. My heart raced. I thought I could hear footsteps outside. This was no dream. Maybe it was the seal? But it didn't sound like the seal.

The footsteps were coming closer . . . somebody was outside – I was sure of it. I heard a twig snap and I froze, my heart banging. I heard a tapping at the door. Then I heard a voice. 'Niilo?'

It had to be a dream. I was hallucinating. I imagined Hannu's voice again, calling me: '*Niilo?*' Part of the blanket fell into my mouth and I felt like gagging. But I was scared to move.

'Are you in there?'

My head spun. What if this was real? I wanted to say something, but the sound stuck in my throat. Then I heard the hut door squeak open. I pulled the blanket down and opened my eyes. It was still gloomy, but a pale shadowed light strayed into the hut. The footsteps creaked on the floorboards . . . I didn't know what to do.

He spoke again. His voice sounded hopeless. 'Niilo?' Like he'd said it a thousand times. Like the last thing he

145

expected was an answer. It was Hannu – I would know his voice anywhere. His voice, now, came out twisted with pain. Then I heard him mutter to himself, 'Give it up, Hannu. He's drowned. Like they said. Accept it.' Then I heard him kick out at something – the cupboard door, I think. 'Why did I teach him to swim? Why? *Why?* I killed him.'

I lay frozen, staring up at the cobwebby ceiling as I heard him drag his feet. Even his feet sounded exhausted. Suddenly I panicked. I was so well hidden behind this box he hadn't seen me. He was going away. He was going to leave the island and I would be alone again. I heard him push the door. I pulled the blanket right down, and the words came out before I thought about it.

'I'm here!'

I heard him gasp. 'Niilo?' I heard his footsteps hurry over the floor. They were coming closer. 'Niilo?' he said again. I heard the flick of a torch, saw the glare of white light. Silvery light beamed over my face, blinding me. 'Oh, my dear God!' That was Hannu.

I blinked up at him, shielding my eyes as he pushed the box aside and fell to his knees. The torchlight swung off and I heard the torch thud on the floor. Then I could see Hannu, his outline dark and shadowy. He was standing over me, his mouth wide open. A pale sliver of light fell on his face. He looked like he was seeing a ghost, or a blessed angel. He looked like he might faint.

'Hi,' I said, not knowing what else to say.

'Niilo? Oh God, Niilo. Is it really you?' Hannu stretched out a hand and touched me on the arm. I felt his wet fingers press into me, as if he was checking I was real. 'It is. It's you. You're alive. Oh dear God, you're *alive*!'

Chapter Twenty-two

I saw a tear roll down Hannu's cheek and glisten in the pale morning half-light. I sat up, feeling really relieved he was there, standing in front of me in this creepy hut.

'I swam all the way,' I blurted out. I felt myself huge with pride. This was the first person I'd told. This great achievement had been locked inside me and now it came bursting out. 'It took me all day. I must have swum fifty kilometres. Or twenty, anyway. I swam the whole day and I wasn't scared.' I suddenly felt really happy. I wanted to talk and talk. I wanted to boast. I wanted to tell Hannu how I had made fire, and gutted fish, caught one even, and how I was brave enough to sleep in a creepy hut. I wanted to tell him everything.

Hannu was shaking his head and staring at me. More tears were rolling down his cheeks. He didn't seem to notice that he was crying, or care. And he was soaked. 'They said you were dead.' He squatted down, took my hand and squeezed it. Water ran off him. 'They said they searched this island three days ago and the other islands around. But they didn't find you.'

Suddenly I remembered that dream soon after I'd arrived, when I was hidden under the bush. Men shouting, and a loud buzzing. So it hadn't been a dream. They really had come looking for me.

'Niilo, they said you had drowned. They found your shoes washed up.'

'I'm not,' I said, which was obvious, but words just kept spilling out. 'I'm alive. I grilled fish and made fire and found berries. I like fish. I like the black charred bits. And I ate dandelion leaves. They got my trainers?'

Hannu nodded. 'They sure did, both of them.' He laughed then, but it sounded like he might cry. 'Oh, Niilo, you have no idea how relieved I feel. I knew it. You're a survivor. Thank God you're okay. I haven't slept, Niilo. I've looked everywhere. I took a boat, said I'd find you if it was the last thing I ever did.'

'You found me.' Again, that was obvious, but it was still a miracle. There are thousands of islands in Finland. Thousands of rocks jutting up in the Baltic Sea. And Hannu came to this one. 'I was waiting for the search party,' I said.

'Believe me, Niilo,' he said, placing his strong hands on my shoulders and staring at me, like he still couldn't believe this was real, 'there was a search party. There still is. They sent out the coastguards. They flew a plane. You've been on the television. Your mother blames herself. Your brother has made a missing-person poster. They lit a special candle for you at the Wild School. And Riku is always down at the shore, looking for you.'

'Really?'

He nodded his head and wiped his tears with his sleeve, then sniffed and nodded again. 'We've all missed you, Niilo.' Then he squeezed my hand and laughed. 'Thank God you're safe. You're alive!'

I sat there on the floor of that hut, with Hannu laughing and crying in front of me, and I thought about Scarface staring out at the sea, looking for me. And I imagined the other boys huddled round a special candle, all saying prayers for me. I couldn't believe my Converse trainers came back. I wondered what kind of poster Tuomas made. We were quiet for a while, me and Hannu. Maybe he was also saying a prayer. Then I heard him sniff and laugh softly. 'Nice place you got here.'

'I got women's magazines for a pillow,' I said, then I laughed too. 'There's some great knitting patterns in there.' I laughed so much I cried, and we were both crying and laughing. I don't know the last time I'd laughed like that. Maybe that was the first time in years? All my muscles ached in a good way. Then, between laughing, I said, 'And I made a friend.'

Hannu lifted his eyebrows and looked over his shoulder. 'Where is he?'

I shrugged. 'I don't think my friend likes it in here.'

'Can't see why not,' Hannu said, switching the torch on

and flicking it around the gloomy hut. He fixed the beam on a mangled bird skeleton. 'Why would anybody not like it? It's a palace.' Then Hannu switched off the torch and grew more serious. 'So, who is your friend?'

Now it was my turn to be serious. I wiped my wet face with the blanket. 'Well, I know it sounds incredible, but . . . my friend is a seal. A huge black seal. It's been watching over me. It gave me fish.'

Hannu shook his head slowly. 'A seal?'

'Yeah, I was scared at first, but . . .' Hannu was still shaking his head. 'You don't believe me? What about all the stories you told me? I'm serious – there was a black seal, and it was looking out for me.'

'Niilo, you swam a long way. Maybe fifteen kilometres.'

'So? You saying I'm making this up?'

'No. I don't know. I mean, you might be . . . I don't know . . . delirious. But what do you mean? It gave you fish?'

'It fished them out of the water and threw them to me. Honestly.' I felt angry now. I knew the seal was real. And Hannu was the one who was supposed to believe in these things. 'I'm not lying! I'm not del—'

'. . . irious,' Hannu finished the word when I let it hang in the air. He looked at me like he was making sure. 'I believe you,' he whispered. 'I'm sorry, Niilo. I've been so worried. I haven't slept. I kept thinking I had found you, under trees, on beaches, in old huts a bit like this one, but then it was a log, or the wrong boy, or my imagination.'

He nodded his head slowly and looked at me. 'I believe you.'

We didn't speak for a while, just both sat there on the floor of that spooky hut, which wasn't spooky now he was there. Then in a quiet voice he said, 'I know this sounds weird, but that huge black seal, I think he guided me here. I've been on twenty-six islands. I thought you had drowned. Or somehow boarded a ship and gone to Sweden like you said you wanted to. I was close to giving up, especially when the wind got up and it started raining. Then I saw this shining black head loom out of the water. He looked at me too, Niilo. It was like he could see right into me. Then he turned round and swam off. I was exhausted. I watched the seal go. My arms were aching – I had been rowing for hours – and the engine was out of petrol. The wind was against me, the rain was lashing down. But the seal stopped, and turned his head to look back at me. It was as if he was waiting for me to follow him. As though he was saying, *Come on. This way!* Suddenly I felt this excitement zip through me. I dipped the oars into the water. "I'm coming, buddy," I said, and pulled back hard on the oars, and followed him, even though the weather was wild.' Hannu smiled. He was still dripping wet but it was like he was shining. 'I followed the seal. I got the feeling he wanted me to stop at this island.'

'Yeah, that's my seal. That's my friend.' Again I felt this huge happy feeling glow inside me. 'It understands me.'

'So do I, Niilo.' Hannu looked at me. It felt the same

as when the seal had looked at me, when I had imagined trees and snow and stars and bears and this mighty great feeling pulse away inside me. I felt this huge smile break open my face, like time stopped. But as the pale dawn light trickled down through the hole in the roof, I saw Hannu's face, saw how worried he looked. I saw the way he frowned and bit his lip. 'So trust me when I say this – but I need to take you back to the Wild School. They are dredging up the sands around the island, Niilo. The marine rescue is still out. Divers are looking for your body. Your family are worried sick. We have to go back, Niilo.'

I felt like I had been punched in the stomach. How could he do this? 'What about my freedom?' My voice came out all choked up. 'I know how to survive. This is my island. I made fire.' I felt my eyes well up. 'I want to stay here. I know how to look after myself.'

'I know you do, Niilo. You've been away four days. That's already a great achievement. Believe me, Niilo, you can feel proud of that. But you can't stay here. And . . . they're blaming me.'

'So you want to take me back there so you'll feel better. So they'll stop blaming you?'

'That isn't the only reason, Niilo. You can't stay here. You know that. And your family are really anxious. Believe it or not, they really do care about you. And they want you to be happy.'

I couldn't believe that. What about what *I* wanted? I wanted to be that mime artist on the Helsinki esplanade, with a hatful of coins to spend. Or the dark-eyed accordion player, spilling out sad and wild tunes. Suddenly it was like I could hear those tunes.

'Like I said, Niilo, real freedom is in here.' Hannu tapped his chest. The accordion music stopped.

I wanted to live my way. I didn't want people telling me what to do. I wanted to go where I wanted. I felt all that pounding away inside me like a drum, but I stared at him and nodded. 'Of course I know that.' I could hear the cold edge creeping back into my voice. 'Do you think I *don't* know that?'

So we left the hut, and I wasn't sorry to leave that gloomy place. The sun was already rising, the rain had stopped, but there was a chill in the air and clouds around. I didn't say much, didn't know what to say. I was leaving my island. I had been the king of this place. But I was hungry. I had been hungry for days. And I had a sore stomach. Maybe it was that tomato soup?

I looked over my shoulder for the seal but I couldn't see it as Hannu and I tramped over the springy heather and the ferns. We skirted the circle of birch and pine trees and came down to the beach and to the sea. Darts of red light bled over the sea's horizon and I saw Hannu's small boat, bobbing a few metres out. He had secured it with a rope looped around a stone. It wasn't much of a boat. It had a tiny outboard motor, but it didn't have a sail.

'Is that it?' I said, and couldn't hide the disappointment from my voice. 'You mean, *that's* my rescue mission?'

'No,' Hannu said. He sounded tired now. I heard him take a deep breath. 'No, Niilo. Your rescue mission is vast. Planes. Coastguard boats. Divers. Police. It's quite elaborate, to be honest. But I was the one who found you. Me and my small boat.' Then he gestured towards it. 'Let's go.' He waded out into the sea and pulled at the rope. His boat jerked and floated towards us. 'Hop in, Niilo,' he said. He tried to smile at me, but could hardly manage it and I didn't smile back.

I knew I couldn't stay on this island, eating fish and berries and sleeping in a horror hut, and I knew I was thirteen, and when you're thirteen you don't have much choice about what you do and where you go, but I had plans inside me. Big plans. For now, though, I stepped forward, waded through the shallow water and clambered into Hannu's boat. It rocked wildly.

'Sit down,' he said, pointing to a bench. He fished out a thick blanket from under a tarpaulin and handed it to me. I sat down and wrapped myself in the blanket. Then Hannu uncoiled the rope and the boat glided away from the island. 'This doesn't exactly fill me with joy,' he said as the boat pushed out to the open sea. 'I mean, taking you back to the place you escaped from.' I looked at him but didn't speak. I could feel the cold hard mask sitting over my face again. 'But I don't know what else to do,' he said. 'Trust me, Niilo, this feels like the right thing. It'll all work out for the best.'

'Oh yeah?' I was enjoying his discomfort. It must be a real pain to be an adult, and have to do the right thing all the time. I ignored Hannu, turned my head and looked back at the shrinking shape of my island. For a while we didn't speak. He rowed and I watched my island get smaller and smaller. 'Niilo's Island.' Then I changed my mind. 'Seal Island.' I thought I had said it inside, but I must have muttered.

'What's that?' Hannu said, leaning towards me. He lifted the oars and looked at me and everything paused. Water dripped off the wooden oars, back into the sea. Hannu tilted his head to the side. 'What did you say, Niilo?'

So I said it, louder, almost defiant. 'Seal Island. That's what I'm calling it.' I would come back one day. I could still see the silhouette of the island and felt a pang inside me. I'd only been there three or four days, but it felt like weeks. So much had happened there that I felt like I was leaving a part of myself behind. Or, maybe, I had *found* a part of myself. Then I swung round to face Hannu and said it again. Except I didn't say it, I shouted it. 'Seal Island!'

And that's when something hit the boat. We both screamed as the boat pitched, lurched forward, and capsized.

Chapter Twenty-three

I plunged into the water. Sea was over my head. I shot up, gasping, and I saw the bow of the boat lift into the sky. Then the sea fell over us again.

Hannu was in the water, his hand reaching towards me as I sank. The weight of the blanket around me was pulling me under and I was thrashing through the water, screaming. My mother screaming. Father screaming. The other boy screaming, then gone. The dream rushed into me. The other boy had been beside me. He had always been beside me. Then he was gone. The sea took him away. Sea water crashed over me and I wanted to give up . . .

I sank and let the water swirl over me. Hannu yelled. He thrashed madly in the water and grabbed me, but I pushed him away. The other boy was gone. What was the point? What was the point of anything? I kicked.

So many people.

Drowning.

The seal.

The black seal was here, in the water. It looked at me – we were both under the water – and memory slammed through me. The seal's face was so close, and everything was suddenly clear.

I could swim. I knew how to swim. I pushed back the sea and swam. I had to find the boy, the other boy. I dived down into the swirling ocean, but Hannu caught me and pulled me up.

'I have to save him,' I gasped, breaking the surface and spluttering, my voice a heave of water and agony.

'I've got you,' Hannu cried, panting. 'It's okay, Niilo. I've got you.'

'But I have to save him,' I cried.

Hannu was strong. He steadied the rocking boat and lifted me half out of the sea. 'Save . . . who?'

'My brother.'

Hannu cried out suddenly as the black seal loomed out of the water. It was so close I could have touched it. 'It's crazy,' Hannu yelled. 'That seal, my God, he's trying to attack us.' Hannu had a hold of my arm. With his other arm he reached for the rocking boat and pulled the lip of it down hard. 'Get in!' he shouted, hoisting me up from the water and pushing me into the boat.

I fell forward into the boat, rolled over and stared up at the pink sky as the boat rocked wildly. The seal dived under the water again. My heart raced. What had I just said? I felt stunned as the image of my brother flashed into my head.

Not Tuomas. This was *another* brother. This brother

158

looked exactly like me. This brother was part of me. And the sea took him. I stretched my arms out, as though I could catch him and hold him tight, but the image vanished. He had gone, like he had before.

'What . . . what happened?' Hannu gasped. He heaved himself from the water and clambered into the boat. He fell down beside me. 'Jesus, I don't know what happened.'

I lay on the deck, still in a dream, still thinking about my brother. I was only vaguely aware of Hannu beside me, panicking and panting, and freaking out as he tried to stop the boat from rocking. He held the sides of the boat and peered over the side. 'God. What . . . did we hit a rock? Jesus, where's that mad seal? Did you see him, Niilo? I thought you said he was your friend? My God, he almost killed us. He's mad.'

But the seal wasn't mad. It wasn't mad at all.

Hannu swung round and looked at me. I was still lying on the bottom of the boat, like I'd been struck by lightning. 'Jesus, are you okay? Are you, Niilo?' The boat was still rocking like a demented cradle and Hannu patted the boards of the hull. 'No leak? Amazing. God, Niilo' – he looked round at me, his face bewildered – 'that seal capsized the boat. I think. Or maybe it was a rock? Or something else? I mean, seals don't do that. Jesus . . .'

But I felt calm. Underneath the racing pulse and near-death experience, I felt strangely peaceful. It was like a film suddenly came on in my head. Or scenes from a film. And it had a title, that film: *Niilo's life!*

'A family in a boat,' I mumbled, dazed. 'A small boat. A storm at sea. There was somebody like me in that boat. The wave snatched him. And there was a man. He had black hair. He tried to save the one like me. My brother. My brother drowned. They *both* drowned. And I was left in the boat with a woman screaming.' I was muttering this. I couldn't help it.

'Oh God,' Hannu cried. 'Look!' The oars were floating away from us, like twigs. 'We need the oars,' he shouted, staring at the floating-away oars. 'There's no petrol left in the engine.' I could see his mind race. What if the seal was crazy? Or what if it had been a shark? Should he dive overboard and fetch the oars?

'It's okay,' I said. 'It was my seal. It won't hurt you.'

'He tried to drown us, Niilo. What do you mean, he won't hurt me?'

Then I slipped overboard before Hannu could stop me. The water felt cool as I swam after the oars. I glanced back and gave Hannu the thumbs up. But he wasn't looking at me. I followed his gaze and there it was again: the seal. It glided through the water and swam next to me. I've heard of people swimming with dolphins, well, I swam with a seal. I saw how it tucked its flippers into its body then, to slow down, how it spread them out and made slow circles. We reached the oars and the seal opened its jaw and carried one in its mouth. I tried to swim back using one hand, and dragging the second oar with the other. That was hard. The seal swam ahead and reached the boat in seconds. I saw Hannu bend over and scoop up the oar. He didn't seem so terrified now, just stunned. Then the seal swam back to me and bit into the other oar to carry it in its mouth over to the boat.

When I clambered back in, Hannu looked like he had been struck dumb. With shaking hands I saw him secure the oars into the oar-locks, but he didn't start rowing. The seal circled the boat three times. I knew it was getting ready to leave and I felt something like a stone crack in my heart. It looked straight at me, that seal did, then turned around and swam away.

'It knows.' My voice had fallen into a hushed whisper. 'It's like the seals in your story. It knows me, Hannu, better than I know myself. It's given me the story I lost . . .'

Hannu dipped the oars into the water and nodded his head. He rowed slowly as the sun came up in the east. 'The seal that watched over you – I'm sure it was the same seal that guided me here. But why? Why did it tip us over? Why, Niilo?' The sea flashed pink and red.

I took one of the oars. 'Remember how you said your dad gave you your past? Remember he sat by your bed and told you who you were?' Hannu nodded. 'Well, I think it's like that.' I smiled at him. I felt like a wise man suddenly, all peaceful. 'The seal knew we wouldn't really drown. It pushed a forgotten memory open, like a door that was locked – I don't totally understand it. You're the one always going on about magic, and mystery. Well, it's a kind of magic.' My voice came out calm and strong. It was like after four days on my island I had a glimmer of how animal magic worked. I felt magical myself.

Hannu seemed to relax then. We were both still wet and I had lost his blanket in the sea. But the sun was getting warmer and drying us and I felt warm, and strong. Hannu dipped his one oar deep, then pulled back. I copied him. I would row with Hannu. The two of us sat side by side on the wooden bench in the middle of the small boat and we rowed. I didn't even think about where we were going. We were just rowing over the sea in the early morning. We were quiet, concentrating on rowing. Sometimes we lifted the oars and took rests. As we journeyed over the sea the story that the seal had given me came clearer. It felt like a jigsaw, fitting piece by piece. It was the story of my life and it wasn't a pretty story.

Maybe Hannu saw the way I was feeling, the way I'd fallen silent. Pulling the oar through the water and looking ahead he said, 'Want to tell me the story?'

I tried to get words to come out, but my throat wouldn't work. By tipping our boat the seal had broken open my lost story, but it wasn't a happy story. Why did I need to know a story that was so terrible? 'It was a long time ago,' I started, my voice like a dry whisper. Hannu leant closer and we stopped rowing. 'I nearly drowned,' I whispered. 'I didn't, but two people did.'

'Who were they, Niilo?'

I answered without thinking. How did I know? Where does buried memory come from? 'My dad and my twin brother.' That's what I said. My head reeled, as if I was in a trance. I imagined the yellow eyes of the seal, like two suns rising over the sea. 'At least, that's what I think. I don't know.'

My hands slumped down and the oar dropped from my hand. Hannu reached over to take it.

Chapter Twenty-four

Hannu rowed over the sparkling sea. I could see the Wild School island now. It started as a dent on the horizon, then grew bigger, like a stone, then a boulder, a huge rock. I could see the chimneys of the building. I swallowed hard. What would they do to me? What would they say?

'I thought it might be something like that,' Hannu said eventually. Then, looking out to sea, he murmured, 'Some people have scars on the outside and some have them on the inside.' He lifted the oars then and let the boat drift. He looked round at me and nodded and I saw how tired he was – he had dark patches under his eyes. 'When I first met you, Niilo, I knew you had lost your story.' Then he took up the oars and dipped them into the water. 'I didn't know what your story was, but I guessed it was a hard story to carry. Those are usually the ones we forget. Or bury deep.'

I let him row. I felt in a daze, but weirdly light. Weirdly

okay. The island came closer and I could see the trees and the pier and the track that wound up from the pier to the school building.

'Oi! Niilo!'

I swung round and peered towards the island. I could see the red-brick chimneys of the Wild School building. There was someone on the pier, waving.

'It's Riku,' Hannu said, then nodded. 'You have a welcome party.' And the smashed glass inside my chest melted into butter, and I felt happy. I waved back.

'Hey! Yo! You're alive!' Riku yelled. 'It's Niilo. He's back! He's alive!' By this time more boys and staff had gathered on the pier. They started clapping. I felt like a celebrity, except tears were running down my face.

'He's alive! He's alive!' they were all chanting.

'They missed you, Niilo. Didn't I tell you?' We were almost there. It was coming too fast. We'd reach the stone pier in no time. Okay, there might be a welcome party. There might not. But pretty soon Hannu would leave. I knew he would. And I would be left on the island. But suddenly that didn't feel like the worst thing in the world.

'Where did you get to?' Riku was shouting. Then he ran through the water, kicking up a huge spray. He reached the boat and cheered, then under his breath said, 'The grease saved you. You're *alive*.'

I laughed. I couldn't wait to tell him all about it.

'Riku is a good guy,' Hannu said, as the boat bumped against the bottom. 'Bit of a wild child, but that's no bad thing. You and him should be great friends.' Hannu was manoeuvring the boat in towards the beach.

I remember what one of the staff members who had come to collect me – Sam – had said the day I came to the Wild School. He had called me 'wild child'. I used to think that was a bad thing, but now it felt like something mysterious and exciting. I jumped over the side of the boat and waded ashore with Riku. He slapped my hand high-five, booted up more water and whooped. 'Good to see you alive,' he yelled. 'What a hero! You did it. Wow!' Then at the shore other people crowded round.

'Thank God you're not drowned, Niilo. Welcome back,' said Marko, the woodwork teacher. 'Welcome back to the Wild School.'

Staff and boys jostled round me. They patted me on the back. So many admiring wide-eyed faces were staring at me. Gaping at my torn shorts, ragged brown shirt and cut feet. 'He didn't drown!' 'Niilo's back!' 'He's alive!' 'Hannu saved him!' 'What happened?' 'Where has Niilo been?' 'Did the rescue plane find him?' Their questions clamoured in my head. Elbows pushing to get a better look. Then I saw the boss man stepping forward and the boys clearing a path for him.

'We are so glad to see you alive and well. And you, Hannu, thank you. You said you would find him, and you did. Welcome back to the Wild School, Niilo,' the head teacher said, reaching out to shake my hand.

I took his hand and shook it. I knew what was coming next.

'Make the most of it, Niilo.'

Chapter Twenty-five

I got a kick out of the awe that the staff and the other boys felt, knowing I had swum sixteen kilometres. (So I was told.) No great punishment was doled out, though lots of counselling sessions. Hannu only hung around for an hour or so, just enough time for a quick meal. It wasn't exactly a welcome feast, but I was so ravenous I would have eaten salty porridge.

Of course Hannu was hailed as the real hero, but I heard how the boss said it would be much better for me if he quickly took his leave, how I'd become over-attached and stuff like that. 'I'll see you soon, Niilo,' Hannu had said before the ferry took him away that very same evening. 'And if you and your family want to come to the wedding, you'd be very welcome.'

I waved and waved, watching his ferry grow smaller and smaller, and a feeling of emptiness fell back into me. At that moment a low honk sounded on the breeze.

Aarne, my new key worker, came up and stood next to

me. 'I love the wild song of the seals, don't you?' he said softly.

The seal honked again and the lonely feeling went. The black seal had come to the Wild School island - I *knew* it was him. Something lit up inside me and I felt a whole lot better. I would see Hannu again. Maybe I would go to his wedding? And the seal hadn't disappeared like I'd thought it had – it had come all the way to the Wild School. It was still watching over me.

Me and Aarne walked up the track, through the pine woods and back into the main school building. 'Welcome back to the Wild School,' Aarne said, holding the door for me. I waited for him to pipe up with, 'And make the most of it,' but he didn't. He went with me along the echoing corridor to my old room. When we got there I couldn't believe it - sitting like they were waiting for me, just by the door, were my red Converse trainers. 'Seems even your shoes missed you,' Aarne said. 'We found them washed up on the beach.'

I grabbed them and laughed. They were faded but still tied together. I looked around my little room. I had only been gone four days, but it felt like four months. Nothing had changed but it all looked so different. I said so to Aarne.

'It's you, Niilo,' he said. 'Nothing's changed here. You have.'

The very next day, my mum turned up. She was hugging me and I couldn't believe how emotional she was being.

Every time I looked at her I imagined her screaming and holding me tight in a boat . . . a long time ago. My forgotten story kept throbbing in my head and I knew there were things I needed to ask her, but sitting in the office didn't seem like the place for storytelling. I was kind of stunned anyway, seeing her suddenly turn up at the Wild School, and didn't really know what to say to her. She just kept gazing at me and saying, 'Thank God you're alive.' Then she went off later on the staff ferry, saying she would see me very soon, and how my brother missed me, and my father missed me. After she left, in a whirlwind, I felt a bit sad.

In the Wild School I had some explaining to do. Plus, there was some kind of payback scheme drawn up. The Finnish government had spent thousands of euros searching for me. So what was I going to do for Finland?

I had no idea. Swim in the Olympic Games maybe? But that wasn't what they had in mind. *Community service* was what they meant. In other words: work. I told them I was only thirteen. Old enough, they said, to work in the fields. So off I went again. But it was different this time.

They put me in a team with Riku. He mucked about. He made faces behind the staff's back. He spat, and swore and winked at me. But in between that, he worked, and so I did too. It was okay. I pulled a few weeds and harvested a few carrots and onions. 'Me and you are best friends,' he said, biting into a bright orange carrot.

'Niilo, you are one serious hero.' The way he said it, like he was making a speech, made it sound absolutely true.

'I would have died of a heart attack without the grease, though,' I told him. I could see how he looked proud about that. How he had been part of my escape.

'Yeah, I know,' he said. 'And I didn't want you to die. Because you and me's best pals.' I couldn't help grinning at that.

Hannu must have put in a word about the drumming because I joined the Wild School band and, like you can imagine, it's pretty wild. I thrash the drums till I'm sweating, and Riku – who is the singer in the band, and into techno punk – says it's great having no neighbours. Nobody tells us to shut up!

Then there were the endless sessions of sitting in circles. Usually it was a riot. Boys broke chairs. They yelled. They punched at leather bags swinging from the ceiling. And we had to do these breathing exercises. But I didn't need that stuff. I was fine. Sometimes I told the other boys stories, about seals and dolphins and magic elk pounding over snow. They said I was a brilliant storyteller now, because I'd survived four days in the wild on my own. I had survived the real Wild School, they said and looked at me like I was some kind of superhero.

But the staff still wanted me to sit in circles and talk all the same. 'So, Niilo, would you like to tell us three things you don't like about the Wild School.'

I could have given them thirty. 'We're stuck here. We're forever picking berries. We can't get off the island. Everything's organised. We have to talk about our feelings. We have to put up with stupid folk. Like, some boys are seriously deranged here. And there's no computer games. We only get to watch a film once a week, and they're baby kind of films. And we have to—'

'Thank you, Niilo, that's fine,' Aarne said. 'And what about three things you *like*?'

'Like the berries,' I mumbled.

'Thought you said you didn't?'

'I said, I didn't like *having* to pick berries. I don't *mind* picking them, but I don't like that I *have* to do it. There's a difference. Do you get it?'

'There's no need to be cheeky, Niilo. Yes, I get the difference.' Aarne took a deep breath, and carried on, 'So, anything else you like?'

I made him wait, before admitting I liked the films on Friday night. Some of the films. Not the really babyish ones. Aarne nodded, and waited for a third like. 'I learnt to swim,' I said, and grinned.

'You sure did. And you like that?'

'I like that. I'm skilled at that.' I gazed out of the window, at the clear blue sky, and thought about the seal. I wondered where it was. I had heard it howling in the night. I had lain awake half the night listening to the seal. When the boat had overturned, that seal had broken open my lost story. Now the image of the boat and the sea and the

172

screaming was never far away. Whenever I closed my eyes it was there. I had a story, but it was vague, like a dream. And though Aarne was an okay guy, I couldn't tell him about it. So I tried to piece it together in my head, like a jigsaw, but so many pieces were missing. The sound of Aarne's voice pulled me back. 'What?' I said, blinking at him. I must have zoned out. I shook my head. 'Sorry,' I said. 'What did you say?'

'Your mother said you could go home for two weeks' holiday. She'd like you home, and your father and brother really want to see you. And we really encourage our students to take holidays, to spend time at home if they can. That's a good thing, isn't it, Niilo? To go home? And when you return to the Wild School, you can join the swim team.' Aarne smiled across at me. 'If it's fine with you, you'll be taken home tomorrow morning.'

So soon? I felt my chest tighten at the thought of going home. Back to the sterile house, Mum's weeping, my dad's cold silences, my brother's successes. But this wasn't my dad – well, I didn't think it was. Maybe somewhere I had always known that? Now I felt it deep down inside. I'd had a real dad, and a twin, and they had both gone. And my mum hadn't told me, or maybe she had always been trying to and I had never wanted to hear. If there was any reason to go home it was to find the other half of it – to get the truth. I was ready to listen now.

'How do you feel about going home?'

'Home?' I shrugged. I felt a shiver shoot up my spine.

Where was home? My island had felt like home. 'Dunno,' I muttered.

'If it doesn't work out you can come straight back here,' Aarne said. 'Okay?'

I shrugged again. 'Okay,' I said, but it didn't feel okay.

That night I couldn't eat dinner, even though it was fried chicken, and even though I sat next to Riku and he kept nudging me and accidentally on purpose spilling salt all over the table. I felt my insides knot up. After dinner I didn't join in with table tennis but sat at the side, biting my nails down to the quick. I watched Riku play and he was a devil at table tennis. I just sat and chewed the ragged skin around my nails. Riku slammed the table-tennis ball into my lap. 'Give me a game,' he said. Ordered, more like.

I shook my head. I wasn't a great player.

But Riku yanked me up and thrust a bat into my hand. 'I serve first,' he said, and next thing I was at the end of the green table with this little white ball flying towards me. Miraculously my bat hit the ball. It sent the white ball flying back. That was a fluke. The next few shots I missed. 'Flick your wrist,' Riku yelled, 'like you do with a flick-knife.' Not that I had ever flicked a flick-knife, but I didn't tell Riku that. I hit it that time, and I liked that *pop-pop* noise of the ball. 'Hey! You're ace at this,' Riku yelled, and we were soon hitting it back and forward hard.

I could feel this red seething anger rise up through me and I smashed that ball so hard. Why did they lie? Even knowing a really sad story is better than not knowing. It's better than having no story at all. I whacked that ball.

A crowd had gathered around the table. Clucking Boy was clucking away. Everyone else held their breath. Somebody was counting . . . fifteen, twenty. We went to twenty-seven, then Riku slammed it so fast off to the side that I missed. The crowd cheered. Riku had won. He galloped round and round the green table with his bat in the air, whooping like mad. I was exhausted. But inside I was on fire. And I knew in that moment that more than anything I wanted to know the truth. I wanted my story. All of it.

Before I went to bed that night I blurted it out to Riku. 'Do you get the feeling that you lost a story? I mean, your story? Like – there's stuff about yourself nobody's telling you.'

He looked at me. His scar wasn't so scary. His dark eyes weren't so hard. He nodded. 'Like, finding your wild song?'

How did he know that? Was he psychic? My heart missed a beat. 'Yeah, yeah . . . that's it,' I said, practically stammering. Then I suddenly got it. Hannu had been Riku's one-to-one worker before me. It all made sense. 'Yeah,' I said again. 'The wild song.'

Chapter Twenty-six

The next morning, early, I was on the boat with Sam and Matti, the ferryman. It was August now, and apart from my four days' escape I had been on the Wild School island nearly four months. My insides were in knots thinking about going to Helsinki. Matti cracked a few jokes as we set off. Maybe he saw how nervous I was? 'Hey, Niilo, want to dive overboard and swim alongside the ferryboat?' But I didn't laugh. I had gone quiet again and said nothing. Sam suggested he give me some peace, so Matti's jokes quickly dried up and we crossed the sea to Helsinki in silence, apart from the screaming gulls above and the throb of the engine.

After half an hour or so, the skyline of Helsinki with the huge copper dome of the cathedral came into view. It wasn't long after that Matti moored the boat at the market square and bade farewell to me and Sam. 'Have a good holiday, Niilo,' he said.

It was still tourist season and crowds were milling around

the market stalls. The market was in full swing, so everything felt busy and noisy. I recognised the stall holders,
even the stuff they were selling – I knew it all so well. I
looked around in a daze, feeling Sam's hand gently gripping my forearm. What did he think? That I would take
off and pilfer a few tourist pockets?

Sam steered me through the crowd and on up towards
the bus station. Music from a raw saxophone echoed down
the street and I pulled back to listen and Sam let me. The
aching sadness of the music cut right through me and I
heard it like I'd never heard it before. It seemed another
lifetime when I had been king of this market square, zipping
up and down these streets, listening to street performers,
doing a bit of business, and going to see a horror film if
I felt like it.

'Seponkatu?' Sam asked when the tune faded. 'That's
the name of your street, isn't it?'

I nodded, but it seemed like a foreign country. Seponkatu!
It wasn't my street – it had never been my street. Maybe
I slept there, that was all.

'We better get on.' Sam steered me up the busy esplanade
and over the road to the number six bus stop. He had
done his homework – the metro would have been quicker,
but it would be easier to escape on the metro. And now I
was famed as an escape artist. But he had no idea . . .
escaping was the last thing on my mind. As we stood at
the bus stop Sam said, just to make small talk, 'So, Niilo,
what number on Seponkatu?'

I didn't bother to reply. Sam knew perfectly well it was Seponkatu, number 39. Just then the bus pulled up. Sam paid the bus fares. 'One adult,' he said to the driver, 'and one child.' Still with his hand on my arm he steered me down the bus aisle and into two free seats. I flashed my eyes around the bus, scared I might see someone I knew. But then I felt this strange empty feeling inside. I knew no one, not in Helsinki anyway. I knew a few people in the Wild School. I had a best friend in the Wild School, but here I knew no one.

The bus took off and I pressed my face to the glass, smudging my nose down flat and peering out. Helsinki rolled past – the busy centre, the high stone buildings, the park, the lake, the statues. Happy people, walking or cycling. People who had their story. They carried it around inside them, knowing who they were, where they were from. I swallowed hard, thinking of my mum, and what would I say to her? How would I come out with it? As we journeyed through the suburbs there were more trees and fewer big buildings, fewer people.

We were nearly at our stop when Sam rummaged in his jacket pocket. 'Oh, I nearly forgot,' he said, pulling out a white envelope. 'This is for you.' He thrust the envelope into my hands. 'It's a wedding invitation,' he said, 'from Hannu.'

I stuffed the envelope into my jeans pocket.

The bus drew to a halt, the brakes hissed and the doors opened. 'Our stop,' Sam said, attaching himself to me like glue and manoeuvring me off the bus. It felt like for ever as we walked up leafy Seponkatu. Twenty-seven, twenty-nine, thirty-one . . . 'Your mum's at the door, waiting,' Sam said, though he didn't need to. I could see her, standing in the doorway, her blond hair lifted up from her face. Sam paused for a moment and tightened his grip on my arm. 'We'll keep checks on how it's going, Niilo. If it doesn't work out, we'll come and get you. But hopefully it'll be fine.' He turned to face me, nodded and smiled. 'Have a good holiday, okay?'

I nodded. Already my mum had started to wave. Then I glimpsed my dad, hovering in the hallway behind, like Security. I felt secretly pleased that my own mother looked nervous of me. It was pretty clear she didn't know what to expect – how I was going to be. Neither did I, but I knew I had changed. And I also knew that the man there with the blond hair who I had always thought was my dad *wasn't* my dad. Suddenly the image of the black seal flashed into my mind, and for some reason I felt better. My heart stopped kicking as I stepped towards the house. I took a deep breath.

'Wave to her,' Sam whispered in my ear. I lifted a hand and moved it mechanically through the air. We were halfway up the path that led to the front door. Like the time I had overturned the table in the canteen, time shifted into slow motion. Each step lasted an hour. I saw my mum falter in her step towards me; I saw the lines at the corners of her eyes. She seemed older. I saw the red dots on her white dress, the dark roots in the yellow-blond of her dyed hair . . .

I felt my mother's hand clasp my shoulder. 'Welcome home, Niilo.' She reached out to give me a hug, but I tensed my shoulders and she must have felt that. She stepped back. Then a shadow darkened the path and my father was there next to her. Except it wasn't my father.

'Welcome home, Niilo,' he said. 'Thank heavens you're safe and well. That was quite an adventure you had.'

I said nothing and Sam cut through the awkwardness. 'Now then, a few formalities. It won't take long,' he said. 'Just a few papers to sign. And I'll be off. Nice place you've got here.' And the attention shifted away from me. Dad was eager to talk to Sam about the garden, the squirrels and the hares that were frequent visitors, and how his youngest son loved leaving titbits out for the animals.

Meanwhile Mum was talking twenty to the dozen, like she did when she was nervous, and in company. The four of us moved up the garden path and into the house, like a babbling river. 'We didn't change your room. Left up your posters. All these funny bands you like. Tuomas can't wait to see you. They're letting him away from school early. Then I thought we could go to the swimming pool later. Fancy that, you turning into a swimmer. Of course, I won't go in, to the pool, I mean, but Dad said he would go in with you. Course, it won't be the same. Same as in the sea, I mean . . .'

I still hadn't spoken, not since leaving the Wild School.

I didn't think Mum noticed though – she couldn't stop speaking, or gazing at me, half laughing, half crying, shaking her head like she couldn't believe I was in the house, standing in front of her. I hardly heard what she was saying – her words just washed over me. It was *my* words I wanted to get out, but I didn't know what to say, how to start. I sat down by the kitchen table and still she was chattering on. 'You suit a suntan, Niilo, you really do. You've only been gone four months but I swear you've grown. You're almost as tall as . . .' I looked up at her. She hesitated and looked down at her hands that she was wringing together. 'A man.' She looked up and forced a smile. 'Something to drink, Niilo? I made some fresh lemonade.'

Sam had gone. Dad was in the garden, but assured her he was close in case he was needed. Mum seemed glad to have a task, even if it was just pouring glasses of lemonade. She fussed around the kitchen, opening and closing cupboards as though she wasn't sure where things were. 'Nice man, that Sam,' she wittered. 'I knew . . . you'd be in good hands. Oh, Niilo, I was at my wits' end. Thank God they found you. Thank God you came back.'

I still hadn't spoken, and I knew that made her nervous. I scanned the kitchen, noting that the hole in the wall, where I had punched it, had been filled in. I stared at my mother as she stirred sugar into the glasses of lemonade and carried them over to the table.

She put the glasses on the table, then hurried over to

the fridge. 'As this is a special occasion . . .' She opened the fridge door and bent down, obviously trying to manoeuvre something out of the fridge. 'Da-da!' she sang as she stood up and swung round, stretching her arms forward to show the enormous cake she had baked. 'It's your favourite.' Her voice was breaking. 'Chocolate cake, with strawberries and cream.'

I looked at her, expecting her to burst into 'Happy Birthday' and me, a little boy of two years old, with my whole life ahead of me, would bounce up and blow out the candles. But there would have been two cakes then, wouldn't there? Because once upon a time I had a twin, didn't I? And she didn't tell me, did she? For a second I felt a stab of emptiness.

She lowered the cake onto the table, letting a nervous smile pull at her face. I didn't smile back. I coughed and continued to stare at her. It's called intimidation, and I do it well. She coughed too, as if it was catching, then swung round to the drawer, tugged it open and fumbled about. The noise of metal clanging against metal rang out. I stared at her back, then watched her take up a large cake knife. She turned round and faced me, a flash of fear across her face, and I saw her eyes flit for a moment to the garden, as if she needed to know she had protection from me, her own son. She coughed again and lifted the knife in the air, letting it hover above the uncut cake.

'Mum?'

She paused, the knife a few centimetres from a dome of

cream. She smiled and this time it didn't looked forced. When had I last called her 'Mum'? Tears smarted her eyes. She slid the knife into the cake. 'Yes, son?'

'Who drowned?'

Chapter Twenty-seven

'What?' She didn't look at me, but at the handle of the knife. 'What?'

So I said it again. 'Who drowned?'

'What are you talking about, Niilo?' She cut the cake. Shakily she put a large slice of cake on a plate and pushed it over towards me. Fat strawberries rolled off the top of the slice. I saw a mask sit over her. I knew that mask so well. *Don't rock the boat*: that's what it was called. 'I don't think anyone in the neighbourhood drowned,' the mask said. 'Not that I know of.' Her voice had taken on a cold hard edge. Impatient. 'I mean, we thought *you* had. I was so worried I couldn't sleep, couldn't eat. I hope you enjoy the cake, Niilo. I wasn't sure whether you would get cake in your new school.'

'I'm not talking about me. I'm not talking about the neighbourhood. I've got this weird feeling – like you're hiding stuff.' My voice was quiet and my throat hurt. Back on the bus I had pictured myself yelling and shouting and demanding the truth. Now all I felt was sadness. 'I mean, something happened to us a long time ago. What happened? People drowned. Who?'

I saw how she turned nervously to check on her husband's whereabouts. Earlier she had needed to know he was right next to her. This time, I guessed, she needed to know he was out of hearing. 'What brought this on?' She tugged at the band holding her hair up and her dyed blond hair fell down around her shoulders. It made her look wilder.

'Maybe I'm crazy,' I said, then the words broke like a burst dam, not shouting, but fast, feeling if I didn't say it now I never would. 'I have this feeling and it won't go away. Hannu says I've lost my story. I need to know who drowned. Things happened to my head when I was away. Like, memories coming back to me. Drowning memories. Someone drowned. A long time ago. I have this memory, sometimes it's a nightmare. I was in a boat a long time ago and people drowned. Maybe you think I'm mad. Maybe I *am*.' I rose to my feet and I saw her flinch. 'But it keeps coming to me. It won't leave me alone. Who was it?' I was scared I might scream or burst into tears. 'Who drowned? I need to know the truth.' I looked at her, slumped in the chair and anxiously pulling at her hair. Why doesn't she tell me the truth?

She got to her feet and I saw her sway, like she might faint. She held the edge of the table and I heard her breathing hard. Then she pushed out across the kitchen towards the back door.

I saw the knife lying next to the cake. She clocked it too and glanced at me, like she was afraid I might grab it and fling it at the wall. But I just stared at it, knowing I wouldn't do that again. Something had happened to me on that island – something to do with the seal, something to do with swimming, maybe something to do with Hannu and his magic stories – but I knew there were a lot of things I wouldn't do again. I sat back in the chair. She stopped and turned round to face me, and she looked so shaken. I spoke again, slower this time. 'I learnt some things after I learnt to swim. There was a boat, and an accident. There's a story you never told me.'

She came towards me hesitantly, still eyeing the knife.

'Don't worry,' I said. She stared at me warily. 'I'm not a monster.' She was still breathing loudly and holding her hand to her chest. I looked at her, at her dark eyes.

'I'll tell you everything,' she cried, pressing her hands now over her cheeks. 'I tried to, Niilo. So many times I wanted to. You didn't want –'

'Who drowned?' I cut over her. 'Just tell me. Who *am* I? I'm probably not even Niilo. *Who am I?*' I was taking a chance, going on a dream and the thoughts that had flashed into my head when the seal upturned the boat. I half believed I really was mad. I half believed the whole drowning story was made up in my screwed-up brain. Never mind the Wild School. Next thing, I could be carted off to hospital. But the other half believed it was true. It was that half I listened to. 'Tell me my story,' I said.

I sounded calm. I sounded strong. I remembered my face reflected in the black pool.

'You are *Niilo*.' My mother took her hands away from her face and I saw fingermarks pressed into her flushed cheeks. 'I'll tell you everything,' she said again.

My whole body was trembling. And though my heart was pounding I was going to listen. I'd taken a risk. Nightmares. A seal. And a feeling deep in my gut. I sat back and stared at her.

She twisted the silver ring on her finger. 'After it happened, I told you.' She was whispering so low I could hardly hear. 'I thought that was the right way, but whenever I mentioned them, you screamed. You clamped your hands over your ears. You couldn't bear it and I felt so cruel.'

'Mentioned who?'

She looked at me, her eyes wet dark pools. 'Them,' she whispered. 'But . . . you were so young, I thought you could start again. And me. So I brought you to Helsinki. It was a long time ago, Niilo. People said how you wouldn't remember. That it was kinder that way. Kinder to forget.'

'Who's *them*?'

'Oh, Niilo. Don't. When I met Kalle you clung to him. You called him Dad. We had a new family and I thought we could start again, here, in Helsinki. You and me. You cried constantly – you nearly drove me mad – and it was Kalle who calmed you down.'

I felt a jabbing pain below my chest, more painful than

187

the emptiness. Hannu was right, I had lost my story, and here it was, after so many secrets and lies, coming back to me. I felt like houses were falling around me. Pillars crumbling. Windows smashing. Ceilings falling in. 'He's not my father, is he?' I felt my throat close up. I nodded to the garden.

'Not in the blood sense, Niilo. But in every other sense he is. Kalle took me in. He took us in. We were poor souls from up north. We had lost everything. I needed to give us another chance, Niilo. I needed help. He loved us.'

'So my father drowned?'

She groaned, like someone was ripping that groan out of her throat. 'Trying to save your twin brother.'

So the visions were right. The buried memories and dreams and nightmares were real. I stared at her. I imagined the seal, remembered how I felt swimming with the seal. I imagined the hands of the seal. And other hands, the ones I always dreamt of. Small hands, drenched with water.

'You should have told me . . .' I felt like I was melting. I wasn't thirteen. I was three.

She was holding me now, holding my hands. 'It happened when you were two years old. We don't remember things that far back. We lived in the far north of Finland, up by the Arctic Circle. Your father often took us fishing – he was half-Sami – and you loved going fishing with him. We had a small boat. The weather was calm. The Baltic was still. You asked to hold an oar. Your father laughed and said you would grow up to be a great fisherman like your grandfather. You held an oar with me, and your brother held an oar with Papa.'

'What was his name?'

'Your father's name was Nilse.'

'And my brother? My twin? What was his name?'

'Isku. You loved him so much, Niilo, and I thought I was the luckiest woman in the world – I had two wonderful children, my beautiful boys. By the end of that day I was the unluckiest.' She was sobbing softly now, but kept speaking through the flow of tears. 'It was a freak wave, Niilo. It came from nowhere. It came over their side of the boat, snatched at their oar. One moment Nilse and Isku were there, laughing and rowing together. The next moment they were gone.'

'My father drowned?'

'Yes.'

'And my twin brother drowned?'

She nodded. I had so many questions. 'Lapland. We . . . we're Lapps?'

'Your father had Lappish blood. I went north as a young woman to work in a hotel. That's where I met your father. So, yes, the north is in your blood, Niilo. But listen to me – I did what was best for us. Please understand. Helsinki gave us a home.

'You took me away. You made us different.' I let go of her hand and took a step back. 'Why did you not tell me? Why did you not tell me I had a twin?'

189

'Believe me, I did try and tell you – but you couldn't bear it. So I blotted it out. I tried to start over.'

I was thumping my chest like my twin was right inside me. 'Why?'

'Stop it, Niilo. Do you have any idea how painful this is for me? I wanted us to start again. I thought it was for the best and maybe I was wrong. Not a day goes by when I don't remember.' Tears coursed down her face.

The story filled the room, like a reindeer: strong, northern. And the feeling of smashed glass inside me wasn't there any more. In a bizarre way I felt strong. It was better to have a story, even a terrible story, than to have no story at all.

We were quiet for a while, then she reached out and touched my arm. 'Who has been talking to you? Was it someone from the village up north? Word got around, of course, though there wasn't even a funeral – the bodies were lost at sea. There was some bad talk. Some cruel people saying it was my fault. Saying I shouldn't have allowed young children out in the boat. Who told you, Niilo? *Who?*' Hysteria rose in her voice.

I didn't know what to say. A seal? The sea? My dreams? Hannu's stories? Or that empty feeling inside? I looked at my mother twisting her fingers together, sobbing silently. I could say I had found my birth certificate that she always said was locked away safely. I could, but I was done with lies. I was done with pretending. 'A seal told me,' I said, 'and bad dreams.'

190

And she nodded, like it wasn't completely weird, like she remembered her first husband and how he would surely say such things. He would tell her about a time when wild animals and wild dreams could tell us things. A faraway look had come into her tear-stained eyes.

'You should have told me,' I said. 'When I was a bit older. I would have been proud.'

'I thought the truth would have killed you. I fled to the south, Niilo, with you in my arms. I gave you a new story. Kalle was good and kind to us, and agreed it was for the best. He adopted you as his own, Niilo. Don't you understand? We had a new family. And for a long while you seemed content. It was only these past two or three years when you . . . you . . .' Her voice trailed off. She took a deep breath and then stretched her arms out towards me. 'But you're right, Niilo. You can be proud. Your father was a strong man. He loved you both.' Then she hugged me and I let her.

I felt a deep wild peace flood through me. I hugged her back. I was proud.

And I had my story.

Chapter Twenty-eight

In Seponkatu 39, they moved around me differently. They didn't avoid me. Tuomas was always gazing up at me and smiling. 'I made this to help bring you back,' Tuomas said, showing me the poster he had pinned up in all the local shop windows. 'It's a good photo of you, eh, Niilo?'

It wasn't, but I nodded. 'I was only about ten in that photo,' I told him. Which was around about the age he was, I guessed. Or maybe he was nine? I looked at him, then looked at myself in the mirror.

'We look alike,' he said.

That wasn't true either, though there was maybe some similarity in our jaw and noses. He was my half-brother – I knew that now, and so did he. Mum had bravely sat us all down the night before and told the whole story. About her first husband, Nilse – my father – and my twin, and the far north of Finland, and the boat. And the accident. Tuomas had come up and hugged me after that. And in a strange way, it was all okay.

I ruffled his hair, liking him, 'You're not as handsome as I am,' I said, with a joking mood in my voice, which was a new thing. I always knew I had a sense of humour locked away somewhere, and these days it was beginning to come out. Tuomas laughed. Even if it wasn't funny, he would have laughed. The truth was out, and it was like everyone could suddenly breathe. 'We're half-brothers, remember?' I told him. 'And I have Sami blood, which you don't.' Tuomas looked at me, wide-eyed. Since my island escape I'd got a lot of wide-eyed admiring looks. 'Want to go out on the skateboard?' I said to him. Of course he did. Mum bit her lip and let us. This was new. She'd never trusted me before.

Tuomas was pretty good fun. And there were loads of things I could show him. I had this amazing sense of balance. Thief training isn't *all* bad. I had learnt a lot of stuff – like stillness, patience, judgement, speed, invisibility, balance. I told Tuomas all about the circus skills workshop at the Wild School. I didn't tell him about me going mad and swinging the stilt around. I made the Wild School sound like this exclusive super-cool place for amazingly talented people. I told him I might train to be a mime artist. 'I wish I could go to the Wild School too,' Tuomas said.

'Yeah, I bet you do. We do woodwork, and nature stuff, and they take you out to study the stars and the planets, and you get to milk the goats, and climb trees and go on assault courses. You work outside, and make things. It's cool.' I couldn't believe it, but I was looking forward to going back.

I had been three days at home. I hadn't smashed anything. Mum and Dad and me had this serious talk about the stealing. 'Would I be able to return the money to where it came from?' they asked me. I shook my head – the tourists would be far away by now – so we sent the money to charities and it felt like a huge relief.

I hadn't slunk out into the town centre to follow my old pursuits, and I promised I never would – the drive I used to have for that was gone. Mostly I did skateboarding with Tuomas, or showed Mum how to make strawberry jam. I think she did know how to make it, but she made out like she didn't. 'That's great, Niilo,' she said, licking the spoon and saying how it was the best strawberry jam she had ever tasted. Sometimes I just sat around the kitchen in a daze, eating and getting used to this new sensation. It was as if the aching emptiness was no longer there. Sometimes I caught myself humming an old tune, or smiling for no reason. Mum too seemed younger, like a weight had been lifted off her. We went to the bookshop in town and brought back books on the Sami people. We looked at pictures. I felt a strange shifting inside. It made me restless, but not in the old way.

At night I leafed through these books. At the Wild School I had got used to thumbing through books, and I liked it. Just gazing at these snowy northern landscapes took me to a different place. Sometimes my fingers trembled so much I could hardly turn the pages. I pored over the pictures of the Sami people with their high cheekbones – a bit like mine – their dark hair, also just like mine. Okay, I wasn't full-blood Sami, but you could see a similarity. Hannu had noticed it.

The Sami lived in the snow. They lived with reindeer. They wore colourful embroidered clothes. And they sang. It was that that kept me awake till dawn. Yoiking, it was called. Hannu had first told me about the y*oik* – the wild song that was a part of you, a deep part. It was the song that knew you, even when you had forgotten who you were. I read that you are given your yoik by someone who knows you well, somebody who understands the yoik. And every yoik is unique, as every person, plant and animal is unique. Even the sea, apparently, has its yoik – its wild song. But so many people have forgotten the songs.

The Sami people live closely with nature. They know it in the way modern man knows his car. They understand how all creatures of the world are linked together, and when those links are broken the world suffers. People suffer. Loads of what I read was in the past, though. The old traditional Sami way of life has mostly gone. The quad bike has replaced the sleigh, and modern music and television have replaced the yoik. And I felt sad. Because I know what it's like to lose something that really matters.

The old custom of yoiking is still practised, I read, but nothing like as much as it used to be. The Sami would have a yoik to heal the reindeer, the tree, the elk, the ocean. 'When you yoik a person they remember who they are. When you yoik the sea,' a Sami elder said in my book, 'the sea remembers its origin.' Reading about the wild song stirred something deep inside me and I felt ancient. Older than the mountains. Older than the lakes. 'And when you yoik a person they remember who they are.'

I lay on my bed with the Sami book open on my chest. A shiver crept over me and I saw long roads and deep snow. I saw forests and iced-over lakes. I saw stalagmites in yawning caves. I saw myself on a long journey, in search of the forgotten wild songs. The vision faded and I saw the lead singer from CrashMetal stare down at me in the dawn light as the book slipped off my chest and fell onto the floor.

I let it fall. I didn't need books any more. I had always known I was different. But up until then I had always felt it in an awkward lonely way. Now I felt it in a strong proud way. Things had changed. *I* had changed. Sure, I would go back to the Wild School soon. Maybe I would be there till I was sixteen. This urge to take off into the wide world soon as I hit fourteen had left me, or at least changed. The Wild School *was* the wide world. And as far as schools go it is kind of funky. Mum says I can come home every weekend. She says the Wild School isn't a prison – it's an alternative kind of education – and I don't have to go if I don't want to.

But Riku says he's my best friend.
And I can visit Hannu and Saara.
Maybe, one day, I really could swim for Finland.

Chapter Twenty-nine

I only had three days left of my holiday. Soon it would be time to go back to school. But there was something to do first, something important. The tenth of August was the date. Three p.m. was the time written on the wedding invitation. I had handled that invitation so much that the red love-heart on it with the names 'Saara & Hannu' had my fingerprints all over it. Mum said she and Dad and Tuomas would really like to come with me. Part of me wanted to go alone but part of me wanted to go with my family. And that was a first. 'Okay,' I said. And it really was okay.

I wanted to wear my jeans and T-shirt, but Mum bought me a cool grey suit. It looked pretty good so I wore it. Tuomas said I looked fantastic. Dad said I was handsome – I had decided I would still call him Dad, even though now we all knew he wasn't really. We drove down to the market-square harbour and parked the car, where the ferry for Suomenlinna was waiting. I wasn't scared of ferryboats now. I saw how Mum bit her nails, though – she was terrified.

'It'll be okay,' I said, smiling at her as we filed down the pier and over the ramp. It was a still day and the sea was smooth as glass. 'It's only a half-hour trip, Mum. You can always sit inside if you want.' And that's what she did.

Tuomas and I hung over the rails, ducking when the gulls dive-bombed. 'When I first went to the Wild School,' I told Tuomas, shouting over the *chug-chug* sound of the engine that we were right next to, 'I was sick all over the place. You wouldn't believe it. I felt like I was going to die.'

'So did I,' Tuomas yelled, his blond hair flopping over his eyes with the sea breeze. 'I really thought I was going to die when you went to the Wild School.'

I ruffled his hair, but felt a lump in my throat. Just then a gull swooped down, screeching and trying to jab at a bit of sandwich that was on the deck. Tuomas grabbed hold of me for protection. 'It's okay, Tuomas,' I said. 'They'll come pretty close but they won't hurt you.' I took him over to the other side of the boat so we could get away from the gulls, and see the island.

'Island ahoy!' Tuomas called out.

But it wasn't the island I saw. I looked out to sea and straight into the yellow eyes of the black seal. 'Look, Tuomas,' I yelled. 'Look at the seal.' Tuomas cheered and waved to the seal. It nodded its head, then flipped back its tail fins and dipped under the water. 'Maybe it's going to the wedding too,' I said.

The ferry blew its horn. I stroked the invitation in my pocket, and when the boat slowed down and chugged alongside the pier, putting down its ramp, Tuomas, me, Mum and Dad were the first to leave. We were caught up in a sea of people rushing from the ferry and onto the island. Soon, though, the crowd thinned out as people drifted off in different directions and it was just Mum, Dad, Tuomas and me, all looking really smart and walking up a dusty path that wound its way across the island. Mum was still looking a bit pale.

'You survived,' I said to her.

She nodded and smiled at me. 'You're right, Niilo. I survived.' Then she sorted her hat and smoothed down her jacket and we all walked together over the cobbled path.

Suomenlinna is a strange place, full of forts, cannons and dungeons. The whole island is a fortress, or it was a couple of hundred years ago – now it's a tourist attraction. We caught sight of cute little red love-heart cards stuck to stone walls, saying *Saara & Hannu*.

'Look,' Tuomas yelled. 'That's them!' We followed the red love-heart cards under a stone archway, round by a little café and past a big church. It was like a 'find the wedding' game.

My heart was racing. I felt nervous and excited, and really glad I wasn't on my own. 'Looks like we'll be there soon,' Mum said, sounding a bit breathless from the walking uphill. 'It's so good he's getting married. I want to thank him so much for finding you,' she said, 'and for being such a wonderful teacher to you. And a friend.'

'Sixteen kilometres has got to be a record,' Dad said. He was also puffing a bit – it was a pretty steep climb. But there were no cars on this island, just bikes and walkers. We marched over a bridge, Mum singing a little love song to herself, to 'get in the mood', she said. The whole island was quaint and historic, and singing in the street didn't seem out of place.

We were heading for a place called Kuninkaanportii: King's Gate. I took the invitation out for the umpteenth time and read the address, but of course I didn't need to – I knew it off by heart. We were getting closer and I saw a few other people hurrying up the stone path that led to King's Gate. I heard the sound of a guitar. The tune twanged out. We all heard it and slowed down at the same time.

'Here it is,' Mum said, and we all went through the huge stone archway that led into the gate. We came into an open green space surrounded by stone ruins. It looked gothic and might have been a great setting for a horror film, except all the white flowers everywhere made it beautiful – and romantic, Mum said. At the far end, near the ruins, there was a crowd of people, all in smart clothes. There were seats in rows and people were filing into the seats as the guitar played. 'Let's sit at the back,' Mum murmured, and we all slunk into the last row.

At the front stood Hannu and Saara.

'They look beautiful,' Mum whispered.

The guitar music stopped and it looked like they were getting ready to speak a poem or something to each other – I'd never been to a wedding before. Hannu was wearing a cream-coloured suit and his dark hair hung loose past his shoulders. He and Saara were holding hands. Beside them stood a man in a white suit – maybe he was the priest? Hannu and Saara were speaking some words now, and their voices murmured over the crowd, but I couldn't make out what they were saying. Then the guitar started again and I saw Hannu scan the crowd. He was looking for me, I know he was. Then he found me. He winked, and his face broke out into this huge smile as I smiled back.

'He's spotted us,' Mum whispered and I grinned.

The wedding went on with poems and music and they swapped rings and people cheered, and I felt fine. After that part of the ceremony Hannu and Saara walked through the crowds of people. There was clapping and cheering as they began to speak to all their guests. Saara looked beautiful, like a queen with flowers in her hair and a flowing cream-coloured dress on.

Hannu made a bee-line for me. He shook my hand, shook hands with Mum and Dad and Tuomas, thanked us all for coming. Saara kissed me and said it was so great we could all come. 'The honoured guest', that's what they called me.

After the ceremony we all took a walk in the King's Garden. People drank wine, and me and Tuomas got sparkling grape juice. Hannu introduced me and Tuomas to his friends. The boss – Mr Stubble – was there from the Wild School. 'It's the boy who swam sixteen kilometres,' I heard people say.

'Yes, it's Niilo,' Hannu said, as though that said it all. 'And with him,' he added, 'is his brother, Tuomas.' People spilled confetti over Hannu and Saara and some of it fell over me. I felt like I was getting married too.

Maybe I was, in a way.

Chapter Thirty

The musicians struck up and the dancing began.

Saara danced with me and said I looked so handsome. Mum and Dad whirled around the dance floor. Tuomas found a girl his age to dance with. Lots of guests asked me to dance, and I managed it fine, even though I didn't know much about dancing. Then in between dances people flocked round me and asked me about the island, and swimming, and making fire, and sleeping on my own under the stars, and was it true that I survived four days alone on an uninhabited island?

Time flew by. I almost forgot the presents. When there was a break in the dancing I found Hannu and Saara over by the chocolate and strawberry fountain. We dipped a few strawberries in chocolate and Hannu winked at me – I bet he was remembering the days we spent picking strawberries. I was! I laughed, licked the chocolate off my fingers and fumbled about in my pocket.

I had two presents. I fished out the little book of poems

called *Arctic Sunrise* from inside my jacket – Mum had suggested that. From another pocket I brought out the wooden carving I had found in a tourist shop in Helsinki. 'These are for you,' I said, 'and Saara.' Then suddenly I didn't know what else to say. I glanced down at the little wooden seal and wished I had made it myself. I would make it much better, and I thought how when I went back to the Wild School I would make wooden seals in the woodwork studio. And I knew exactly what they would look like.

Saara took the seal and kissed me on the cheek. Hannu took the book. 'I love this,' he said.

I swallowed, then ran on with my prepared speech. 'Um, congratulations, and I hope you two will be really happy.'

Then Mum appeared, all flushed from dancing, and told Hannu what a great influence he had been on me, and she wanted to thank him from the bottom of her heart. 'I've got my beautiful son back,' she said, and hugged me.

When the food had been eaten and the musicians took a break, a few people strayed outside to watch the moon over the sea. Saara was chatting with Mum and Dad and Tuomas. Hannu sat with me on a rock, looking out to sea. There were a few gulls around, hoping for crumbs.

'Thanks for coming, Niilo,' Hannu said. 'It means a lot to me and Saara. And it is great to meet your family.'

I shrugged and wrung my hands together. 'That's okay,' I muttered.

'It's more than okay, Niilo.' Maybe it was the effect of the champagne, or it being his wedding day, but Hannu said how I was like the boy he had been – the one he had forgotten. I tried to imagine what that was like: you have a car crash and you lose your youth and all the memories of being young. 'It's like you are a part of me,' he said. 'And I don't want to forget any more. I don't wish for you to forget any more either.'

And I told him everything my mum had told me. About the boat accident, and my dad, and my twin brother. I told him their names: Nilse and Isku. And we stared out at the huge yellow moon glittering over the dark sea. It was like Nilse and Isku were there, swimming in the sea. Maybe they were swimming with the black seal. Maybe they were together in the great ocean holding hands – my dad, my twin brother, and the seal.

Behind us a door opened and the low rift of a saxophone reverberated over us. Then Hannu said, 'You're okay now, Niilo. Whatever happens now, you'll be okay. You have your story. You know where you are from. And you survived four days on a deserted island. And you have made friends with a seal. You are getting on with your family. From now on in it just gets better.'

I laughed. I knew he was right. 'I made friends with Riku too,' I said.

'That is so good,' Hannu said. 'He could do with a friend like you. And, you know, the Wild School isn't so bad. As far as schools go, it's pretty amazing.'

'So, I should make the most of it, eh?' I said, laughing. I had already decided that was exactly what I would do.

'Hey, people,' someone shouted from a group of guests that had drifted outside. 'Come in and dance! They're playing a midnight love song!' Saara laughed and I saw her take my mum by the hand. I watched them head back to the restaurant, where the dancing was.

'I'll be with you soon,' Hannu shouted back.

I wanted to keep this moment a bit longer. I could sense Hannu getting ready to stand up, so I blurted out, 'Remember how you spoke about wild songs? You called them yoiks?'

'That's right,' Hannu said. 'I found my yoik. Now look at me, I just married the most beautiful woman in the world. How about that?'

'I was thinking . . . how one day . . . I might go north. I might find some old Sami man to give me my yoik . . .' I looked away and stared out to sea. I didn't know I was going to say that. Now it seemed so real, like all along I had always been looking for my wild song. I imagined the future opening up ahead of me, like a deep adventure, winding far to the north.

'I hope you do that, Niilo. This is just the beginning. You'll travel far. You will find your wild song. I know it. Then you will help others to find theirs.' He gestured to the dark sea ahead. 'The Baltic could do with its song too.'

I stared out to the moonlit sea and thought of my island. I thought of the creepy hut, and the black seal. I thought of Tuomas and his 'find my brother' poster. I thought of my mum calling me her beautiful son. I thought of Dad saying how he would consider it an honour if I called him Dad. And I thought of the nightmare I had had for as long as I could remember, and how it had turned into a dream where a boy just like me tumbled down through the water, and turned into a black seal, and a man who drowned trying to save him somehow turned into a man called Hannu who came to work at the Wild School, with his stories, and his crazy notion of teaching me to swim in the sea.

'Thanks, Hannu,' I said, turning to look at him. 'You really helped me.'

'It works both ways, Niilo,' Hannu said. 'Thank you.'

And we sat like that for a few minutes longer, me and Hannu on a rock, listening to the deep song of the sea. Until a door swung open behind us and the sounds of the party spilled out into the night.

Saara stepped up behind Hannu and put her hands over his eyes. 'Guess who?' she whispered.

'My wife,' Hannu said, laughing.

Just then hands slipped over my eyes too. 'And guess who?'

'Mum,' I said, and I laughed too. While Hannu and Saara walked back to the wedding party Mum sat down on the rock next to me. The moon was glinting silver on the sea.

'It's beautiful, Niilo,' Mum said in a hushed voice. 'I was always afraid of the sea, but it feels so peaceful.'

Just then my seal lifted its head from the water. It was a round black shape in the silver moon path. It made a low trumpeting noise and I heard Mum gasp. 'It's okay,' I said. 'It's watching over us.' Then another seal next to that seal lifted its head from the water. Now two seals were watching us. It felt like the spirits of Nilse and Isku. I was going to say that, but Mum said it first.

She spoke their names – the names she'd kept locked up inside her for years. 'Nilse,' she whispered. 'Isku.'

It felt like a long time we sat there, me and Mum, gazing out at the two seals in the Baltic Sea. The words of Hannu's song played in my head – *everything was going to be all right*. It really felt like that. Then the seals made one long, deep sound.

'That's their wild song,' I murmured. Their song put a shiver right through me. Then the seals flicked back their tail fins and slipped under the water.

I got to my feet then and so did Mum. We turned away from the sea, and there were Dad and Tuomas, standing by the door of the restaurant. They were lit up with sparkling lights and waving to us. 'Hey, Niilo!' Tuomas called out. 'Come and join the party!'

Me and Mum walked together over the grass towards the wedding party. 'What do you say, Niilo?' she said.

I looked at her and smiled. 'Yes.'

A Big Thank You

I would like to warmly thank Creative Scotland for giving me a one-month writing residency on the island of Suomenlinna in Finland. Part of my task there was to foster literary links between Scotland and Finland in children's literature. Finland boasts many vibrant book-shops and children's publishers and is an inspiration in the world of children's publishing. Thanks also to H.I.A.P. (Helsinki International Artist's Project) for hosting and supporting me during this residency, and to the many wonderful Fins I met. Thanks also to Finnish storyteller Yvonne Karsten for reading several manuscripts of *Wild Song*, likewise to Rupert Jenkins. You are two very bright stars!

Finally thanks to my agent Kathryn Ross, and to the wonderful people at Piccadilly Press.

Author's Notes

After reading *Wild Song* you might be interested to find out more about Finland and some of the themes touched upon in this book. The following is a brief introduction to Finland, the Sami people (Laplanders) and also to the Finnish national epic, *The Kalevala*.

Finland

Finland is the most eastern of the Scandinavian countries with Russia to its east, Norway to the north and Sweden to the west. It sits on the Baltic Sea, with the Bothnian Sea to the west. For a long time Finland was under Russian and also at times Swedish occupation, only gaining independence in 1917. Finland has a population of 5.2 million and the southern city of Helsinki is the capital. It is a large country with thousands of lakes and islands and the most forested land in Europe. Finland is known for the midnight sun in the summer and Northern Lights in the winter, for

Santa Claus, reindeer, rye bread, saunas, berries, ice and snow. Its national animal is the bear.

The Sami People

The Sami are the indigenous peoples of the Arctic. The area they live in, and have inhabited for over 2,000 years, stretches from the Kola area in the north of Russia and west across the north of Finland (through the region known as Lapland), and on through northern Norway and Sweden. In Finland there are different groups of Sami, numbering around 9,000 people. Amongst them there are the mountain Sami, the sea Sami, the lake Sami, the reindeer Sami and the river Sami. They speak several different languages. The traditional dress of the Sami – often brightly coloured and trimmed with fur, beading and embroidery – shows where a Sami person comes from. Traditionally the Sami people pursued a variety of livelihoods, such as coastal fishing, fur trapping and sheep and reindeer herding. But the traditional way of life for the Sami people is threatened by competing uses of land. If the government cuts down forests in a reindeer-herding area this destroys the reindeers' habitat. Generations of Sami children were taken away to boarding schools in the past, and the effects of this are still being felt. Today the Sami way of life experiences cultural and environmental threats, including oil exploration in the Arctic, mining, dam building, logging, climate change, military bombing ranges, tourism and commercial development. In Finland today the Sami inhabitants have a right to maintain and develop their language and culture as well as their traditional way of life.

An important aspect of this tradition is the *yoik* – or wild song. The yoik can be deeply personal or spiritual in nature and is often dedicated to a human being, a landscape or an animal – for its wellbeing. Each yoik, sung by a yoik-singer, is meant to reflect a person, animal or place and comes out of the shamanic spirituality that sees nature as sacred and believes that human beings become unwell when we are out of harmony with nature. Shamanic practices, such as singing the yoik, aim to honour and restore that balance between human and nature. The yoik is one of the longest living music traditions in Europe.

The Kalevala

Throughout history people have shared stories. Sometimes these stories remind us of our origins. Some tell of Gods and Goddesses. The actual creators of the Finnish Epic, *The Kalevala* – the 'rune' singers, both men and women, lived hundreds, perhaps thousands of years ago. Their names are long forgotten but in this great epic poem their stories live on. In the 1800s folklorist and collector Elias Lonrot made many visits to Eastern Finland to listen to the stories told by the old Finnish poem-singers. These people chanted their stories of creation in a particular rhythm (trochee) and some chanted their stories while playing a kantele (a harp). Elias wrote hundreds of these poems and stories down and in time put them together and created a national creation epic for Finland called 'The Kalevala.' The stories in *The Kalevala* here are set in Finland's prehistoric Iron Age. They could also be said to be set in a mythic dream place of the imagination.

RUNE THE FIRST

I am driven by my longing
And my understanding urges
That I should commence my singing
And begin my recitation.
I will sing the people's legends,
And the ballads of the nation.
To my mouth the words are flowing,
And the words are gently falling,
Quickly as my tongue can shape them,
And between my teeth emerging.

Some of the main characters from *The Kalevala* are:

Vainamoinen – steady, old, the father everlasting.
Ilmarinen – the master craftsman, the smith who hammers the magical sampo – a Finnish Holy Grail.
Aino – the young maiden pursued by Vainamoinen.
Louhi – mistress of Pohjola, the gap-toothed hag of the northlands.

The characters and stories in *The Kalevala* inspired many works of art, and the book has been translated into forty-five languages. This dream-like and wondrous fantasy epic ends with the words:

> [. . .] *this way therefore lies the pathway.*
> *Here the course lies newly opened,*
> *Open for the greater singers,*
> *For the bards and ballad singers,*
> *For the young who now are growing,*
> *For the rising generation.*

Janis Mackay
Edinburgh, Scotland
December 2014

PRESS

Thank you for choosing a Piccadilly Press book.

If you would like to know more about our authors, our books or if you'd just like to know what we're up to, you can find us online.

www.piccadillypress.co.uk

You can also find us on:

We hope to see you soon!